CW00409975

After years of looking forward to join-
ing her grandfather in the Caribbean,
Amalie had arrived there at last—to
find that he had died, and she was
landed with the job of managing his
schooner charter business singlehanded.
And she was forced to accept the help
of the mysterious Blake—an attractive
stranger who was all too likely to walk
out of her life again as abruptly as he
had entered it.

THE LAST NIGHT AT PARADISE

BY

ANNE WEALE

MILLS & BOON LIMITED
15–16 BROOK'S MEWS
LONDON W1A 1DR

CHAPTER ONE

As the time approached when at last she could return to her lost paradise, to the free and easy sea-going life she had missed almost every day of the five long years spent in England, Amalie found it difficult to conceal her excited anticipation.

For Tabitha's sake she did conceal it, in the same way that, on coming to Europe, she had kept secret her misery at having to give up her first experience of perfect happiness.

Even at fourteen years old, Amalie had had a well developed sense of responsibility, and there had been no question but that Tabitha, two years the younger and of a far more vulnerable, nervous temperament, had needed the security of her sister's presence, if not always under the same roof then at least within easy reach, which would not have been the case had Amalie remained with their grandfather in the West Indies.

The girls had come into his care while their father and mother, both internationally famous musicians, had been on a long concert tour of South America. Up to that time they had usually accompanied their parents, receiving their lessons from a governess and living in hotel suites or rented apartments, a life which, if only subconsciously, Amalie had found as uncongenial as Tabitha had found the year on their grandfather's schooner after the air disaster which had left them orphans.

Although shocked and distressed, Amalie had not felt her loss as deeply as Tabitha. From an early age she had known that her parents were disappointed by her lack of any musical ability.

Fortunately Tabitha had inherited their gifts, but even

so their father had not always been content with the signs
of an exceptional talent demonstrated by his second child.
On many occasions, in one of his difficult moods, he
had made Amalie painfully conscious of her defects. It
was not until she had been living with her grandfather
for some time that she had come to realise that she had
never been defective, merely different. In her grandfather's eyes it was Tabitha who was the oddity; a deli-
cate, fastidious little girl who was afraid of the water and
did not want to learn seamanship for fear of blistering
her hands.

But between John Lawrence and Amalie there had
sprung up an instant rapport. They had found they were
two of a kind, and she had basked in his approval as
happily as in the sun which seemed—at least in her
memory—to have shone all the time they had lived with
him.

She had hoped it would go on for ever; that blissful
new life as what the old man called his cabin girl. But
all too soon it had ended, and she had been obliged to
accompany Tabitha to England where her sister had
been offered a place at a residential school for youthful
musicians. It had been arranged that Amalie should
attend an ordinary boarding school not far away, and
their holidays would be spent in the household of a
middle aged couple who made a profession of catering for children who, for various reasons, needed a home
away from home.

Only once, between the ages of fourteen and nineteen, had Amalie seen her grandfather. He had come on
an unexpected visit to England at the time when she
had been in conflict with her schoolmistresses because
they wanted her to go on to university and become a
career woman, and she had very different ideas about her
future. Her plan for a happy life was first to achieve a
diploma in domestic science, and then to rejoin her
grandfather in the Caribbean, there to take over the cater-

ing side of his charter business.

This had seemed to her headmistress and house-mistress to be a waste of a good brain, but Amalie knew that she was not as bright as they thought her. She had passed her examinations merely because she had worked hard, not because she was clever or ambitious. To apply herself to her studies had been her instinctive way to make the terms seem to pass faster.

Although, in general, parents and other members of the older generation seemed prone to oppose the ideas of people of her age, her grandfather had surprised her by taking her side in the matter.

'If that's what you want to do, m'dear, that's what you shall do,' he had told her. 'You're like me ... know your own mind. My father wanted me to follow him into banking. I knew it would bore me to death, so I ran off and made my own way in the world. It hasn't brought me wealth or importance, but at least I can say I've enjoyed my life, and that's what counts in the long run. I suppose nobody reads Hilaire Belloc nowadays, but he hit the nail on the head when he wrote, "There's nothing worth the wear of winning, but laughter and the love of friends". People who make that their motto may never amount to much in the public eye, but they end their lives with contentment instead of regret.'

A few days later he had returned to the West Indies, leaving his elder granddaughter fortified by the confidence that, as soon as Tabitha was eighteen, she could leave her with a clear conscience.

The younger girl did not want them to separate, but by this time Amalie had realised that Tabitha was inclined to make use of people, including her sister. It was plain that she had a brilliant future as a cellist, and equally plain that, if Amalie allowed it, she could very easily become the factotum in the shadows beyond the spotlight of Tabitha's future fame.

Fond as she was of her sister, she saw no reason to

sacrifice her own plans for her. Apart from the blood-tie between them, they had little in common. Each year of thir development from childhood to young womanhood had shown increasingly plainly that Tabby was like her father—single-minded to the point of ruthlessness where her art was concerned—while her own traits were all from her mother's side of the family.

Thus it was that, not long before Amalie's twentieth birthday, the two girls had their last breakfast together in the flat which they shared with a third girl who was, at the moment, on holiday.

It was a small flat, but conventionally central. Amalie had found it during the first few months of her catering course. Later, when Tabitha had finished her time at her special school and come to London to prepare for her début as a soloist, there had been a room free for her. Now Amalie's room was about to be taken over by a student of textile design, so there was no question of leaving Tabitha on her own, with no one to turn to in an emergency.

Nevertheless, as she looked at her sister's lovely face on the other side of the breakfast table, she was troubled by last-moment doubts about Tabby's ability to cope with the practical side of life.

Their mother had been a pretty woman and Tabby's pale-skinned, heart-shaped face held the promise of even greater beauty. Amalie had the same large grey-green eyes and fair hair, but she lacked the perfection of Tabby's profile, and her sister's air of ethereal mystery.

Amalie's chin was square, her nose slightly snub, and her general appearance healthy and cheerful. No one looking at her would ever guess that, inside this sensible-looking exterior, was concealed a strong strain of roman-ticism.

Tabitha's objectives were acclaim and luxury. Already she spent some of her time gazing in the windows of the great London jewellers, considering how to adorn herself when the time came. Amalie's secret yearnings went beyond the maxim recommended by her grandfather. As well as laughter and the love of friends, she longed to be loved by a man whom she could adore all her life.

But although she sometimes saw men who had something about them which appealed to her, usually they were strangers hurrying through the rush hour crowds whom she knew she would never see again. Or, if she did meet one of them, he would either be attached to another girl, or there would be something off-putting to douche the first promising flicker of physical attraction.

When she looked at herself in the mirror, she also faced up to the fact that, if ever she should meet a man who matched her criteria in every respect, he would be seeking someone as lovely and gifted as her sister, not an ordinary person like herself.

'I think you'll come back,' said Tabitha, as she had many times before. 'I know you liked it the last time, but that was ages ago when you were still a teenage tomboy. It will be quite different now. It won't be a game any more. I can't imagine anything worse than having to cook in that climate. And Grandpa is old ... seventy-four. Supposing he crocks up, and you have to nurse him ?'

'I can think of worse fates,' said Amalie lightly.

These were points they had argued over and over again. She had hoped that, on her last morning in England, her sister would send her off with good wishes instead of doleful forecasts of what might go wrong.

It was almost a relief to say goodbye and set off, alone, to the airport. Her only luggage was a medium-sized suitcase for which she had bought a mini-trolley because it was heavy with books. She was taking very few clothes, knowing that anything made wholly or even partly from synthetic fibres would feel uncomfortably hot, and that she would probably live in bikinis, shorts and tee-shirts, with one or two dresses of cool Indian cotton for special occasions.

The first long lap of the flight, south-west across the Atlantic towards the crescent of islands between Puerto Rico and Trinidad, was an uneventful hiatus between her past and her future. She watched a movie, chatted to the woman next to her, and read magazines provided by an attentive stewardess.

The second lap was less relaxing.

The island which was her destination was served, she discovered, by a small, single-engined aircraft capable of carrying eight people, this number including the pilot who was waiting to greet his passengers by the fold-down steps to the door just behind the port wing.

The first to board was a man who took the seat beside the pilot's. He was followed by a party of four tourists who occupied the two seats with their backs to the cockpit and the two which faced them. There was then another partition with, behind it, two more forward-facing seats, one of them alongside the door.

Amalie settled herself in the seat on the starboard side, and concluded that only six places had been booked on this flight. She would have found it interesting to sit up front with the pilot. However, her seat in the tail had a much larger window than those on a 747 jumbo jet or a Boeing 707 and would give her an excellent view of the seascape below.

About five minutes passed, and the pilot remained on the tarmac, chatting to the full-lipped, soft-voiced island girl who had taken the passengers' tickets and checked their weights as well as that of their baggage.

After several more minutes one of the tourists remarked, 'I wonder what's holding us up? We should be airborne by now.'

The reason for the slight delay became apparent when, out of the door of the departure lounge through which they had emerged a short time earlier, came a very tall man, so darkly bronze-skinned that, at first sight, Amalie took him for an islander.

However, as he strode briskly in their direction she saw that he was deeply tanned rather than naturally brown, and although his hair was black and curly, it was silky rather than wiry like that of a person of African origin.

In London she might have decided that a crop of such thick, tight curls must be the result of a perm. But the man approaching the aircraft was not in either of the age groups which tended to follow the more extreme trends of male fashion. He looked to be around thirty, and not the type who would spend much time on his appearance. He was casually dressed in a pair of clean, sun-faded jeans with a darker blue shirt, and he carried neither briefcase, wrist-sac nor holdall.

'Sorry to keep you waiting,' he said to the two by the steps.

'That's all right, sir. We're only a few minutes behind schedule.'

The pilot boarded the plane before him, then turned in the narrow aisle and waited to supervise the closing of the door.

Before the newcomer entered the aircraft he took off his sunglasses, caught Amalie's eye, and smiled at her. His eyes were not brown as she had expected them to be because of the darkness of his tan and the blackness of his hair. They were as blue as his shirt, as blue as the Caribbean sky.

Something in the quality of his smile reminded her of two lines from a verse by her grandfather's favourite writer, Belloc.

> *His hair is crisp and even curls,*
> *And he is saucy with the girls.*

And the context of the lines made her realise where she had seen his type of hair before: on the heads of waiters in London restaurants which specialised in the cuisine of the lands round the eastern Mediterranean.

Greek men had that kind of hair, and southern Italians, and Turks. Yet there had been no trace of an accent underlying the cultured English in which he had addressed the pilot, and his height seemed uncharacteristic of the men of those countries, as were his vivid blue eyes.

As the steps were drawn up and the door closed, and the pilot went through the routine of explaining to them how to open it in an emergency, the size of the man seated beside her made the plane seem suddenly much smaller.

'You'll find coffee, or cold drinks, in the two cool boxes behind you. Now, if you'll fasten your seat belts ...'

With the same instruction to the others, the pilot made his way forward and soon they were taxiing gently towards the runway.

As a child, Amalie had flown many times without ever feeling fear. But since the crash in which her parents had died, she had dreaded take-offs and landings. She knew that the risk was slight compared with the dangers of road travel, but she could not help tensing with terror as the engine-note rose to full power and the hurtle down the runway began.

She hoped, by averting her face, to hide her alarm from her neighbour, forgetting that hands can be equally expressive. Suddenly, about half way along the runway, at the point where her insides became a tight knot of tension, a hand fell on one of her clenched hands.

When, startled, she looked round and saw the long brown fingers enclosing her small left fist, the man beside her leaned closer and, speaking into her ear because of the roar of the engine, said, 'You don't mind, do you? I'm okay on jets, but these little toy-town machines always give me the jitters, and there being no stewardess on board ...' He left the sentence unfinished, and drew back to give her a teasing grin which successfully distracted her from the chilling thoughts which had been in her mind seconds earlier.

Considering her state of mind before he touched her, and spoke to her, Amalie would not have believed herself capable of responding to any man's magnetism at such a moment. Yet, afterwards, she had no recollection of feeling the wheels leave the runway or of seeing the earth begin swiftly to fall away beneath them.

All she remembered was the comfort of the strong male hand holding hers, followed by a fluttering sensation in the pit of her stomach—a feeling quite different from fear—when his blue gaze shifted to her mouth and then returned to meet her eyes.

She knew then—had known it, perhaps, as his long legs brought him towards her—that here was another of the men who had something about them which drew her. Indeed, where this one was concerned, physically he seemed without flaw.

Able, like most of her sex, to take in all manner of detail at a single glance, Amalie registered that he had excellent teeth, short, well-scrubbed finger-nails, and shoulders in splendid proportion to his inches-above-average height.

Beneath them there was a slight thump as the aeroplane's wheels were retracted. But the hand holding hers did not slacken and, under his continued scrutiny, she found herself starting to flush.

'The others are unfastening their seat belts,' she pointed out, some moments later, and followed the remark by unclipping her own belt.

Perhaps the man was left-handed. At any rate he undid his belt without releasing her hand, and might have held it indefinitely had not one of the party in front of them leaned out of his seat and said to him, 'Could we trouble you for the cold drinks?'

At this he did release his hold, using his right hand to lift the cool box from its storage place behind them. It turned out to be the one containing the coffee flasks. The second box held a variety of canned soft drinks.

'What would you like, Miss Heron?' he asked, when the people in front of them had been attended to.

She thought it was very quick of him to have spotted her surname on the card slotted into her holdall.

'Orange juice, please, if there's some left.'

He pulled the tab off a can, poured the contents into a plastic beaker and added two pieces of ice. 'How's that?'

'Thank you.'

Predictably, he chose a beer. As he raised the beaker to his lips, Amalie noticed his sinewy forearm, lightly veiled by dark hair. His wrist watch was gold, wafer-thin, and of an elegance at variance with his jeans. But there was no chain round his neck, and no rings on his fingers. His feet, not particularly large considering his height, were in canvas deck shoes. She liked his lean, sunburned ankles.

'Are you here on holiday, Miss Heron?'

'No. Are you?'

'No,' he answered.

But like her, he did not volunteer his reason for being on the aircraft.

The inter-island flight did not take long, and soon the aircraft began a gradual descent towards the coral-sand beaches and wooded hinterland of the island which was her grandfather's base.

During the time they had lived with him, his crew had been a young West Indian. But two years ago Sam had been lured away by a tempting offer from the skipper of another boat, and since then John Lawrence had had several temporary replacements, none of whom had sounded at all satisfactory. Reading between the lines of his frequent letters to her—for he was a man who made light of difficulties—Amalie suspected that the seasons since Sam's departure had been harassing ones, and this had increased her impatience to join her grandfather and make life easier for him. Without an efficient mate, the charter business was hard going for a skipper in his seventies.

Close to the island up-currents of heat made the light aircraft bounce. The first time this happened, instinctively Amalie gripped the edge of her seat, and the man beside her reached for her hand.

'It's nothing to worry about. In England this happens when one flies over a motorway or any wide road.'

'Does it? I've never flown in a small aeroplane before.' She hesitated, then, unable to repress her curiosity, asked, 'Are you English?'

'No, but you are, I imagine.'

She nodded, waiting for him to reveal his nationality and introduce himself. It seemed from the mischievous quirk at the corner of his mouth, and the matching glint in his eyes, that he wasn't holding her hand only to reassure her. He gave the impression of finding her as attractive as she found him, and the fact that he wasn't a holidaymaker made her hope that this might be the beginning of ... but the half-formed idea died away as he said only, 'Fasten your seat belt.' Surely if he meant to pursue their acquaintance he would have told her his name, and asked what had brought her to the island, and where she would be staying?

He kept hold of her hand until they touched down, and as the plane taxied towards the small terminal building, he did ask if someone was meeting her.

'Yes, my grandfather.'

For a second or two she considered telling him her grandfather's name, and the name of the schooner. But pride made her contain this information. It was up to him to do the running—if he wanted to. If he lived on the island, probably he had his car at the airport. If the answer to his question had been No, would he have offered her a lift? Eager as she was to see John Lawrence, she could almost regret that she had not arranged to make her own way to the waterfront.

The door of the aircraft carried a notice warning passengers that it must be opened only by the pilot, except in emergencies. As he came to the rear to attend to it, the tall man leaned close to Amalie to give the other man more room. Although she was slender, she was not a petite girl, but he made her feel small and fragile. She could feel his breath on her cheek and knew he was watching her face while she watched the pilot and tried to show no reaction to the disturbing proximity of the man whose broad shoulder was pressing against hers.

Having followed the pilot out of the aircraft, he turned and put his hand under her forearm while she stepped down on to the ground, her fringe lifting off her forehead as a gust of breeze caught the half-curling tendrils.

But instead of walking with her towards the buildings, he said, 'Goodbye, Miss Heron. It's been a pleasure flying with you.'

Then, with a word of thanks to the pilot, he turned and strode off ahead of the rest of the passengers.

As she went through the brief formalities of arrival, Amalie looked about for her grandfather, but could see no sign of him. He did not own a car, and it might be that he had had difficulty in getting a taxi, although it didn't seem likely.

She was waiting for her suitcase to be brought from the plane when, through a window overlooking the airport's car park, she saw the tall man again. Unencumbered by luggage, he was already free to go on his way.

He, too, had had someone to meet him: a woman in tight white trousers and stilt-heeled sandals, with a luxuriant mane of red hair falling down her bare back.

Amalie watched them walk to a sleek silver sports car. He opened the door of the passenger seat for the woman before moving round to the driving seat. Within a few moments he had reversed out of the space and was speeding away, the woman shifting sideways to talk to him so that Amalie did not see her face but only the hand she had laid caressingly on his shoulder, the nails long and fashionably lacquered, several rings on her fingers glinting and flashing in the hot sunlight.

So that's that! she thought disappointedly. Yet another of my brief encounters. Oh, well, never mind. He's probably all brawn and no brain. He can't be too strong in the head to have a wife or girl-friend who wiggles her bottom like that, and wears diamonds with beach clothes.

Yet, while they had been in the air, he hadn't given the impression of being just a splendid hunk of beefcake nor, in spite of his costly gold watch, had he seemed the nouveau-riche type who would like his woman to show off her jewels at all times, and draw other men's glances with the provocative sway of her small firm buttocks.

'Amalie Heron?' someone said.

Amalie forgot the pair in the silver car and turned to find herself facing a tall, rather thin elderly woman with her white hair cut boyishly short, and her pleasant brown face very wrinkled by years of living in a sunny climate.

She offered her hand, saying, 'I'm Angela Scott. I've been a friend of your grandfather's for some years. I think he may have mentioned us occasionally in his letters.'

'Yes, he did. How do you do, Lady Scott.'

Amalie knew that she was the widow of a retired admiral who had also been in the charter business, but who was now dead, his place as skipper having been taken by his son.

'Oh, please use my first name. We're very informal out here, you know, as indeed I believe people are in England now, much more so than when we lived there. Is this all your luggage? Good. Then shall we go to the car?'

'Where is Grandpa? Is anything wrong?' asked Amalie, beginning to feel rather uneasy at being met by a stranger, however agreeable.

'He hasn't been well for some time. He should have cut down the number of charters, and given himself longer breaks in between. A six-month season with forty-eight-hour turn-rounds is far too gruelling for an old man. But men who have always been active often find it hard to accept that they're no longer young, and can't tax themselves and get away with it,' said Lady Scott, as she led the way out of the airport building.

"If I'd realised he wasn't well, I should have come out here sooner. Oh, why didn't he let me know?' said Amalie distressfully. 'Is he *very* ill, Lady Scott?'—forgetting the older woman's injunction. 'Must he give up chartering completely?'

'This is my car.'

Angela Scott unlocked the boot of a small, somewhat battered runabout, and Amalie hoisted her heavy suitcase over the rim.

As she turned to look at the older woman she knew, before Lady Scott spoke, that something terrible had happened.

'My dear, brace yourself. I'm afraid I'm the bearer of very bad news.'

'He ... he isn't dead?'

'Yes. Yesterday morning. He had already had one mild heart attack ... a warning which he disregarded. The second one killed him instantly. It was how he wanted to go, without a long, painful illness. For him it was the best way.... but not for you, my poor child.'

The Scotts had arranged for Amalie to spend the night in an hotel. As was usual in that part of the world, her grandfather's burial had already taken place, but they thought she would not like to sleep alone on the schooner.

'And staying with strangers, from whom one feels obliged to hide one's feelings, is an extra strain. You will be better in an hotel, with me on call if you need me,' explained Lady Scott.

She went on to say that her doctor would prescribe

some sedative tablets if Amalie wished for them, but that she herself did not advise them.

'I feel sure, from my own experience, that it's far better, in the long run, not to try to numb the pain,' she said gently.

So Amalie spent much of the night in tears of grief and regret, but when, late the following morning, Angela Scott came to her room, she was heavy-eyed but composed.

'I thought you would probably sleep late. Would you like to come and have lunch with us, or would you rather be alone? Don't be afraid to refuse if you don't feel like meeting Roderick yet.'

'I should like to come. Thank you. It's good of you to befriend me. It would have been so much worse to be completely alone here.'

'John was always a marvellous friend to us. He taught my husband everything he knew about chartering. They became very close.'

They went downstairs and walked the short distance to where Angela had parked the car. On the way, at a street crossing, Amalie saw the redhead who had met the tall man at the airport yesterday. She was at the wheel of the silver car, waiting for the lights to change in her favour. Her front view was much as Amalie had expected it would be. Her face was pretty in a pin-up calendar style, but her mouth, in repose, had a hint of hardness about it. A tight yellow sun-top displayed, in full detail, the shape of her breasts. The cigarette she was smoking was fitted into what looked like a gold and diamond holder.

Angela must have noticed Amalie staring. She said, her tone dry, 'That young woman is Madame Androcles, the subject of much gossip about here. Your grandfather used to speak highly of old Androcles, but although I strive to be charitable, I can't help suspecting that girl was more interested in his millions than in his qualities.

How any girl can marry a man old enough to be her grandfather is something I shall never understand—although she only had to put up with him for a year. Now, so it's said, she's having a fling with his bodyguard. Still, one shouldn't judge people without knowing the full circumstances. She may have had a wretched upbringing, poor creature.'

So the man on the plane had been a millionaire's bodyguard, and was now making hay with his widow. An expression of distaste crossed Amalie's face as she recognised the weakness of her judgment in finding such a man attractive. She was not sure where rich old men recruited their bodyguards. She seemed to recall having read that the man who guarded the Royal Family were detectives seconded from the police force. But she had a feeling that millionaires were more likely to hire ex-mercenaries and men of that sort; tough, ruthless types who were efficient protectors because, although they operated within the law, they had a good deal in common with the criminals who might threaten their employers' safety.

'I wonder how Grandpa came to know Mr Androcles? I don't remember him ever mentioning him to me,' she said.

'I don't know the circumstances of their acquaintance —only that John would always spring to Androcles' defence if anyone ridiculed him for marrying that dreadful little gold-digger. I never heard your grandfather say an unkind thing about anyone, although, at the same time, he was sparing in his praise of people. He thought very highly of you for sticking it out in England on account of your sister when he knew you would have preferred to be out here. "A very staunch little girl, my elder granddaughter", he used to say of you.'

'Really?' said Amalie, surprised. Her eyes filled with quick, hot tears. She blinked them back, and fumbled in her bag for a tissue. 'If only we could have had just a short time together,' she said huskily.

'Yes, it is a great shame. Obviously you and he had so much in common; whereas his daughter, your mother, was of quite a different temperament and never very close to him, I gather. It's strange and interesting, isn't it, how genes often skip a generation?'

It was not a long drive to the waterfront where the Scott's ketch, *Carrageen*, was berthed not far from the graceful white schooner with *Seafarer* painted on her bows.

'There's an hour before lunch. Would you like to go on board *Seafarer* and see the changes and improvements your grandfather has made in the last few years?' Lady Scott suggested.

Thus it was that Amalie's first sight of Roderick Scott was when he came to tell her their lunch was ready, and found her sitting forlornly in the schooner's cabin, lost in sad dreams of what might have been.

In view of his mother's age, Amalie had expected him to be a man of at least thirty-five or even forty. But he was only a few years older than herself. Either his parents had married late in life, or he had been an after-thought.

At first clearly he was uneasy at having to cope with a girl so recently bereaved. But when he saw she was in command of herself, he relaxed and made himself pleasant. In looks he was very English with sun-bleached brown hair and grey eyes.

It was after lunch, when they were having coffee in the shade of *Carrageen*'s awning, that he said, 'Look, I don't like to bother you with business matters so soon after your arrival, but I spent this morning trying to find someone who could take over *Seafarer*'s first charter of the season in three weeks from now. Unfortunately everyone seems to be fully booked, so there's nothing for it but to wire the bookers and explain why their trip has to be cancelled. I'll attend to it for you, if you like.

It would have simplified matters if your grandfather had booked through a charter broker, as we do. But he'd been in the game a long time, and most of his passengers came to him through the personal recommendation of other satisfied customers.'

'But does the first charter have to be cancelled?' asked Amalie. 'I mean, the plan was that I should join forces with Grandpa. I don't want to go back to England. Couldn't I manage the charter with whoever is ... has been crewing for him?'

'The trouble is John sacked the last man he had at the close of last season,' said Roderick's mother. 'He was always unsatisfactory and, with your arrival on the cards, there seemed no point in retaining him. I think you'd find it almost impossible to engage a reliable crew at this stage of the year.'

'Quite impossible,' confirmed Roderick. 'Which reminds me, your grandfather's will is in the hands of his solicitors—who are also our solicitors. Unless you would rather postpone such things for a few days, I could take you to see them this afternoon.'

'Oh, surely next week would——' began Lady Scott.

But Amalie squared her shoulders and said determinedly, 'No, I think I should tackle these things immediately. There must be *some* way to fulfil my grandfather's bookings. I can't let people down at the last moment. I expect they've been looking forward to the trip for months. They may even have booked the kind of bargain-price flight which I came out on, and in that case they won't get their money back.'

She paused before adding, to Roderick, 'All this—arranging the funeral, and taking me to the solicitor, must be a great nuisance for you at the time when you're in the middle of preparations for your own season. When do you start?'

'In a fortnight, as bad luck would have it.'

'Bad luck? Why do you say that?'

'Because, had your first charter coincided with ours, we could have got over the problem by going out together. I shouldn't think the charterers would have minded, in the circumstances. Sometimes a large group of friends will book a couple of boats. I could have skippered *Seafarer*, with Mother sailing *Carrageen*, and you cooking for both lots.'

'Yes, but we couldn't have gone on doing that all season, so it would have been only a temporary expedient,' answered Amalie. 'There has to be a solution somewhere. It's just a question of finding it. Anyway, I'll spend one more night at the hotel, as I've overstayed the check-out time, and tomorrow night I'll sleep on *Seafarer*. I love the way Grandpa has done out my cabin. I think you must have had a hand in it, didn't you?'—to her hostess.

'Yes, your grandfather wanted to make the cabin rather less spartan than it was before so, when my eldest daughter and her husband came out for a holiday with us, I asked her to bring a few yards of pretty furnishing fabric—it's a Laura Ashley print, as you may have recognised—and I ran up the curtain for the port, and the covers for the bunk and the chair,' explained the older woman. 'I used to enjoy doing up the various houses we had while my husband was in the Navy, but there isn't a great deal of scope for interior decoration on a boat. I thoroughly enjoyed helping John to improve your quarters.'

Amalie's interview with her grandfather's lawyer served only to add to her worries. Having introduced them, Roderick left her alone with the partner who had handled the old man's will and he, after conventional expressions of sympathy, said, 'As you may already be aware, Miss Heron, you are your grandfather's only beneficiary—although I'm afraid that term is somewhat inapposite in this case. I'm sorry to have to tell you Mr Lawrence's estate is heavily encumbered.'

'Encumbered? I don't understand.'

The solicitor removed his spectacles and began to polish them with a piece of chamois leather. After a moment or two, while continuing to polish, he bent a solemn stare on her, and explained, 'The estate consists of the vessel *Seafarer* which is worth a very considerable sum of money. But it cannot be sold and the funds invested because it is, in effect, mortgaged against a substantial loan made to your grandfather by someone to whom he turned for assistance at the beginning of his financial difficulties.'

'I didn't know he had any financial difficulties. His letters gave the impression that his charter business was flourishing.'

'A correct impression,' agreed the lawyer. 'When the loan was arranged—it was then interest-free, I should add—there was every prospect that your grandfather would be able to repay it in the time agreed. However, one foreseeable hazard, and another less predictable eventuality, have conspired to defeat his intentions. In the first place the cost of maintaining you and your sister in England rose far more that he had anticipated, and in the second place the original lender has died and his successors have altered the conditions to include the current, very high rate of interest.'

'But surely my father's estate paid our school fees and other expenses?'

'No, no—I'm afraid not. Your grandfather doubtless wished you to think that, but it wasn't the case. Your father lived to the hilt of his very considerable income and left very little.'

'Oh, God, what a terrible burden for poor darling Grandpa—and he never gave even a hint!' she exclaimed, in a choked voice.

'I'm quite sure he felt his responsibility for you and your very gifted younger sister was extremely worthwhile. The last time I saw him he was full of pleasurable anticipation of your arrival. It was only the altered terms of the loan which were a worry to him.'

'Who was it who lent him the money?' asked Amalie. 'One of his charterers?'

'No, it was a Mr Cheiro Androcles, a very wealthy old gentleman, of Greek extraction as his name suggests, but a citizen of the United States who chose to spend his retirement here. I believe your grandfather met him many years ago at a time when Mr Androcles was the owner of one of the Greek islands and Mr Lawrence was chartering in the Mediterranean.'

'I've had Madame Androcles pointed out to me. She, presumably, is the successor you mentioned just now?'

'That I can't tell you, Miss Heron. Old Cheiro was the patriarch of a large clan of expatriate Greeks, and I've no doubt the terms of his will were widespread and complex. I shouldn't think his young widow would concern herself with any aspects of the estate which were not of direct concern to her'—on a note of sarcasm.

When, half an hour later, Amalie emerged from the building to find Roderick waiting for her on a shady bench in the square outside, her expression caused him to say, 'More problems?'

She nodded. 'You shouldn't have waited. I could have found my way back.'

To her surprise he put his arm round her shoulders for a moment and gave her something between an encouraging hug and an admonitory shake.

'Nonsense. You need someone to keep an eye on you till you find your feet. One of the reasons I like chartering is that the people who do it take a friendly interest in each other's difficulties and try to be helpful. There's a camaraderie among us which you don't find in other walks of life. That's why even my father, who was rather a diehard in many ways, didn't blow his top when I opted for chartering instead of one of the more conventional careers. He knew it was a good life, not just for retirement but for one's working years.'

As they made their way back to the waterfront, Amalie found herself touched and warmed by that brief pressure on her shoulders. Unlike Tabitha, who was by nature un-demonstrative, she had often felt a lack of simple affec-tion in her life. A number of young men had been only too willing to hug and kiss her, but not in a friendly way.

Having explained to Roderick what had transpired in the lawyer's office, she told it again to his mother who was still sitting under the awning, but now had a pair of thick needles in her hands and a ball of white mohair on her lap with which she was knitting a lacy, feather-light evening wrap.

'So what was the upshot?' she enquired. 'What did he advise you to do?'

'I think his private opinion is that I should surrender the boat to whomever now has the lien on it, and go back to England and get myself a job there,' said Amalie. 'He didn't actually suggest it, but I felt it was in his mind. But I'm not prepared to give up as easily as that. I've asked him to find out who the lien-holder is, and then, if it's Madame Androcles, I shall go to see her and ex-plain the position. She may not know that after her hus-band died, his lawyers altered the terms of the loan.'

'I should doubt if you could expect a great deal of sympathy from her,' Lady Scott said reflectively.

'Oh, I don't know,' Amalie answered. 'If, as you sur-mised yesterday, she's been through tough times herself, she might be more sympathetic than old Cheiro's accoun-tants and lawyers.'

'She might, but I feel it's unlikely.'

Amalie had supper with them, and then Roderick walked her back to the hotel where she sat up until after midnight, reading an account book she had found in her grandfather's cabin, and studying his cheque stubs. In conjuction with the facts and figures set out for her by his solicitor, these gave her a fairly clear picture of his income and outgoings, the latter now considerably reduced because her own allowance could be deducted from them. But Tabitha, in spite of the bursary she had won, and the grant to which she was entitled, would still need financial assistance for some years to come.

During the evening meal the Scotts had mentioned a man who coped single-handed with parties of up to four charter guests. But *Seafarer* was equipped to take six passengers, and Amalie knew it was impossible for her to manage single-handed. She had to have some assistance, and that meant that while she could probably keep her head above water and repay the interest on the loan, it was going to take her forever to repay the capital.

Nevertheless she went to bed determined to fight tooth and nail to keep possession of the lovely vessel lying in the harbour. To lose *Seafarer* would be a betrayal of her grandfather's good opinion of her.

Years before, as a flat-chested, coltish fourteen-year-old, Amalie had quickly mastered the basics of seamanship. One of the first lessons she had learnt was that professionals like her grandfather did not hurl mooring lines ashore in the manner of actors and amateurs. To do so was to risk the ignominy of the line falling short of the dock, and possibly fouling the propeller. Either John Lawrence had given her a quiet instruction to pass the first of the two spring lines to someone on the quay, or he had landed her from the stern.

This, and many other professional techniques, she had not forgotten during her years in England. Indeed, by reading the books by all the famous lone seafarers from Joshua Slocum to Dame Naomi James, she had greatly increased her theoretical knowledge.

Waiting for the solicitor to keep his promise to contact her as soon as he had any news, she passed the time by refreshing her memory of the schooner's equipment and stowage. Also she made many enquiries in the hope of finding a crew; but the Scotts seemed to have been right when they warned her that, at this time of year, it would be a wild-goose chase. There were a few men available, but none she judged trustworthy and competent. However, she did not give up hope. ·

On the fourth day after her arrival she was refreshing her memory of the circumstances governing the use of Pan and Mayday signals, when she heard herself hailed, and saw her lawyer waving to her from the quay.

She fetched him aboard in the dinghy, offered him an iced beer, and asked what he had to tell her.

'Nothing hopeful, I'm afraid, Miss Heron. I understand that most of Cheiro Androcles' property passed to his favourite among his many relations, a man called Andronicus Androcles. He, so I'm told, has little need of his inheritance since he is himself a financial genius of no mean order. He has also the reputation of being a great ... er ... ladies' man, so had you appealed to his lenience all might have been well. Unfortunately the lien on this boat has not passed to him but to the widow, Madame Androcles. She, I regret to tell you, is not prepared to review the matter. It may be that she has seen *Seafarer*, which is certainly one of the handsomest vessels in this harbour, and fancies the boat for herself.'

'Have you spoken to her in person?'

'No, only to the accountant who handles all her business affairs.'

'And who may not have even consulted her,' said Amalie sceptically.

'I'm sure he would have done, Miss Heron.'

'I'm not. I don't trust people like that. They have calculators instead of hearts. I'll see her myself.'

'You may have difficulty in contacting her. Paradise, the Androcles' mansion, is not like any other house here. It contains priceless furniture and paintings, and the place is very secure. There's a high wall all round the grounds, and a guard on the gate who admits strangers only if they have an appointment. Probably there are other security measures as well.'

'Well, if Madame Androcles refuses to see me at home, I shall have to try to intercept her when she's driving about town,' said Amalie. 'Thank you for coming, Mr Blunt. I'll let you know how I get on.'

She had feared that the Paradise number might be ex-directory. But although it was in the book, her first call was unsuccessful. She was told—presumably by the butler—that Madame was out. She was still out when Amalie tried again. The third time she rang, she was given a name and number which she guessed to be those of the widow's business adviser.

This, while disappointing, was not unexpected. But when she reconsidered her next step, she realised it might be several days, a week even, before she succeeded in ac-costing Madame, and she couldn't afford to waste time which would be better spent continuing her search for a crew.

After some thought, she packed a grapnel, a coil of strong line, and a pair of stout gloves in a small grip. Then she changed her shorts and sun-top for jeans and a long-sleeved green tee-shirt, and set out to visit Paradise.

A rather ramshackle open bus, with Angel Baby painted on it, saved her a three-mile walk out of town.

As it rattled along, its driver singing, Amalie wondered what the penalty would be if she were caught trespass-ing, and if by doing she was running the risk of being told to leave the island, and of having *Seafarer* confiscated.

She took comfort from the thought that, apart from scaling the wall, she had no criminal intent.

Before the bus stopped, it passed the imposing gate-way which was the entrance to Paradise. The wall sur-rounding the estate was at least ten feet high, and sur-mounted by spiked bars which reminded her of those on the top of the wall round the gardens of Buckingham Palace.

Perhaps half a mile from the gateway, the wall turned at a right angle, leaving the bus route and forming a barrier between the grounds of the estate and a field with a crop which she did not recognise.

About a hundred yards from the road, having made sure she was unobserved, she flung the grapnel, with the line already attached to it, towards the top of the wall. At the second try the flukes of the grapnel engaged with the strong spiked bar, and a few moments later she was dropping into the undergrowth of the shrubbery on the inner side of the wall.

Having disengaged the grapnel while she was perched on top of the wall, Amalie closed her mind to the possibility that the tropical vegetation might be the home of poisonous snakes, and re-coiled the line before stuffing it back in the grip.

This she kept with her while she advanced cautiously through the bushes which became less dense away from the wall. Presently she came to a paved walk. Praying she would not meet a gardener, or a patrolling security guard, she followed the path to a point which gave her a glimpse of the house.

It was a magnificent example of an early eighteenth-century plantation house. She judged the low wings on either side of the main block to be modern additions designed to be perfectly in keeping with the elegant colonnade which formed a verandah on the ground floor, and a wide shady balcony on the first floor of the original building.

After concealing the grip among the low branches of a bush with bright scarlet blossoms, she made her way from one place of cover to another. Unfortunately the house itself seemed to be surrounded by stretches of open lawn, with many sprinklers at work to keep it green and velvety, which she was loath to cross for fear of being spotted.

Having seen Madame Androcles, she would not have been surprised to find the garden had its share of vulgarities. But in fact the ornaments were not modern monstrosities, but mossy antique urns and lead figures of the kind seen in the gardens of stately homes in England. It seemed the dead millionaire's only lapse of taste had been in his choice of his last wife, for presumably he had had at least one previous wife, perhaps several.

Presently Amalie's stealthy circumambulation brought her to a wall of mellow rose-red bricks. She remembered her grandfather telling her that, in bygone times, ships from Europe had used bricks as ballast on their outward voyage to the Caribbean, hence the resemblance of much of the island's architecture to the Queen Anne and Georgian houses in the country towns and villages of England.

Evidently the wall was a screen round a swimming pool. She could hear people's voices, and splashing. How many people? And was Madame Androcles one of them?

At intervals the wall was strengthened by buttresses, from one of which some bricks had dropped out or crumbled enough to provide rather perilous footholds.

Only a little less surefooted than she had been in her tomboy teens, Amalie climbed to the top and peeped over, her head being camouflaged by the tendrils of creeper growing there.

Peering through the leaves, she was just in time to see a man's body cleaving the air between the highest of the pool's three diving platforms and the shining surface of the water.

It was an enormous pool, at least forty feet long and twenty wide, rectangular at the deep end and Roman-shaped at the other. Steps led from the curve into the clear blue of the shallow water. There, lounging back on her elbows, her long legs partly submerged, lay the millionaire's widow. She was wearing an emerald bikini with several gold chains round her neck, another round her waist, and an ankle-chain which Amalie could see glinting under the water.

The identity of the man remained uncertain. Instead of coming up from his dive, he swam the whole length to the shallows under the water, standing up and refilling his lungs with a deep breath which expanded a powerful chest armoured with muscle.

The bodyguard, thought Amalie, having half expected that it would be the man who had flirted with her on the plane.

He did not sit with the widow, but turned and swam back to the steps at the other end of the pool where he pulled himself out and, his tall frame streaming with water, crossed the wide, flagged surround to a group of towel-covered loungers. As he did so, a West Indian manservant appeared through an archway, carrying a tray with a jug of iced fruit juice—or it might be something stronger, a summer punch—and two tall glasses.

From her hidden vantage point, Amalie heard the bodyguard say, 'Thank you, Peter,' and then he took up a towel and gave his thick crop of black curls a brisk rub before lowering himself on to one of the loungers.

At the other end of the pool, Madame Androcles rose and began to walk her undulating walk towards where he lay. The man sipped his drink and watched her coming towards him, his expression impassive.

Watching them both, Amalie wondered who was in command of the relationship; she, because she had the money, or he because she was hungry for a young, virile lover after her year as the wife of a wrinkled old man who probably had had sheepshank legs in place of the long hard thighs of his bodyguard, and a slack paunch instead of the firm, flat stomach of the tall man.

The thought of a relationship based solely on lust,

without an atom of love in it, made Amalie shiver with distaste.

She would have climbed down from her perch and gone round to reveal herself to them, but in the last moment before she began to descend, she saw Madame Androcles reach both hands behind her to pull the strings of her bikini. The gesture made Amalie freeze.

Too late she realised that the moment to speak to the widow had been while the man was in the water. Now, it appeared, there was going to be an amorous interlude which she would have to sit out, and which might lead to their going indoors. Or would they make love there, in the sun, knowing themselves to be safe from intrusion unless they recalled the manservant?

Frozen with dismay and embarrassment, Amalie saw the woman recline on the lounger nearest to his. Obviously she made a practice of topless sunbathing, for her breasts were only a fraction paler than the rest of her voluptuous body.

'Pour me a drink, will you, sweetie?'

The man put his glass on the ground and swung himself back to his feet to fill the other glass for her. All his movements had the lithe grace of someone in perfect condition.

When he handed the drink to the widow, she said, 'And a ciggy as well, please'—indicating the case and lighter she had left lying on the low drinks table.

'Do you want to die young?' the man asked, as he handed them to her.

'Oh, God, you're a cheerful one, aren't you?' Annoyance sharpened her voice, revealing unmusical vowels. 'No cigarettes . . .' she sipped the drink and grimaced, '. . . and no gin. Do you have any vices, one wonders?'

'You know my vice—women,' he answered. 'But being a non-smoker myself, I don't care for lips flavoured with nicotine. And I drink only wine in the daytime. Too much gin before sundown in this climate and you won't keep your looks for long, Stella.'

She gave him a petulant look as she lighted the king-size cigarette she had taken from the gold case. There was defiance in the way she blew out a plume of smoke.

The man shrugged, and said, 'Excuse me.' He turned away, and took a header from the edge of the pool.

Watching him swim away from her, the widow gave vent to an obscenity and began to jab the cigarette in the soil of a plant pot. Then she sprang up and headed towards the archway.

Amalie clambered down, intending to intercept her on the way to the house. Then it struck her that now the widow was in no mood to listen kindly to an appeal from a strange girl. Clearly it was the man who called the tune between them, and while this redeemed him a little in Amalie's eyes, she still thought him fairly worthless to stick around here on any terms.

Reaching the foot of the buttress, she considered what to do now, and decided to skulk for an hour, in the hope that a more propitious opportunity to put her case would occur later.

To this end she concealed herself in a thicket of bushes, and sat watching the house and regretting the chance she had missed earlier on.

She had been in hiding for half an hour when she drew in a sharp breath of panic. A very large black Alsatian had come into view and, although she was not nervous of dogs in the normal way, she was very frightened of this dog in this situation.

Was it a pet or a guard dog? Either way, would it pick up her scent? The thought of the horrible injuries which a large fierce dog could inflict on a man, let alone a lightly clad girl, made her quake with terror.

The next five minutes seemed like fifty as the dog ambled about, here and there snuffling the ground. Perhaps it was merely by chance that it chose to come in her direction, but suddenly, within a few yards of the bushes, its seemingly aimless meanderings changed to alert suspicion of an alien presence somewhere near.

It flashed into Amalie's mind that some time ago she had read that even the beasts of the jungle would, if boldly confronted, retreat instead of attacking. Acting on this, and the feeling that she would rather be mauled in the open where someone might see and intervene than in the dark of the bushes, she scrambled out of the thicket on the side farthest from the Alsatian. Then, another snippet of memory making her fold her arms, she forced herself to walk round and face it.

From the moment the branches had rustled, the dog had begun to bark loudly. When she faced it, the barks changed to growls.

'It's all right, boy ... quiet now ... good dog.' She tried to speak calmly and firmly, but heard her voice quaver with fear.

The Alsatian resumed its barking, clearly a little uncertain because she was moving towards it rather than backing or running.

As it seemed on the point of attacking, a command, in a parade-ground bellow, made its threatening growls suddenly cease, and with the strongest relief she had felt in the whole of her life, Amalie saw the tall man striding towards her.

As she was already much browner, and dressed differently, she would not have been surprised if he had failed to recognise her. That he did, and remembered her surname, astonished her.

'Miss Heron! What the devil are you doing in here?'

'I wanted to see Madame Androcles, but it seems to be rather like asking for a private audience with the Queen, so I—I climbed the wall.'

His black brows lifted. 'Did you indeed? You took a big risk. Prince here doesn't bite people, even uninvited strangers, but you weren't to know that. At night we let loose two dogs which do bite intruders.'

'I don't make a habit of trespassing. I was desperate.'

The vivid blue eyes narrowed slightly. 'Desperate? To see Stella? You interest me. Has she made a pass at your boy-friend? Do you want to tell her to lay off? Save your breath. What she wants, she takes—if it's available.'

'It's nothing like that. Please ... will you take me to her?'

He glanced at his waterproof watch. 'She's probably out, at the beauty parlour; she spends most afternoons there. But we'll see. Come.'

With a beckoning gesture he led the way across the lawns with the big black dog, now looking friendly and harmless, loping at his heels.

On the verandah the dog stopped and sat down, as if forbidden to enter the rooms within. The verandah itself was furnished like an outer drawing-room with groups of sofas and chairs and large low glass tables.

Amalie followed the tall man into what appeared to be a study, judging by the desk and the book-lined walls. On the deck was a row of telephones, one of them a house phone with a battery of press-buttons. He lifted the receiver, touched one of the buttons and, while he was waiting, looked her slowly up and down.

His scrutiny made her aware that she was no longer as neat as when she had set out. Indeed she was scratched and dishevelled, sticky with the cold sweat of fear, and her jeans must have ripped on a thorn, for there was a three-cornered tear above her left knee.

'No answer. Not in her room,' he said, after an interval. 'She won't be back for at least two hours. Meanwhile you look as if you could do with a drink and a shower. What's your tipple? Whisky? Gin and tonic?'

It was on the tip of her tongue to say *I thought you didn't approve of spirits before sundown.* But she curbed the remark, and said only, 'A little rum, if you have it.' She remembered her grandfather giving her rum for a cold. She had never liked any other spirit.

'I should think we might run to that. This way.'

They left the study by the inner door, and crossed the hall to the foot of the butterfly staircase. With her hand on the curl of the polished mahogany newel post, Amalie checked. 'Where are we going?'

'Upstairs, for your shower. What's the matter?'

'I don't think I should. Madame Androcles might not like it.'

'It's not her house now.'

'Oh, isn't it. Then Mr Andronicus Androcles might not like your encouraging strangers to make use of his house. I can have a shower when I get back.'

'Back to where?'

'To my boat in the harbour.'

He shrugged. 'As you please, Miss Heron. But your punctilious standards will allow you to swallow a tot of Mr Andronicus Androcles' rum—yes?'

'Yes, I don't think he would mind that.'

They entered another of the rooms on the ground floor, this time a small sitting-room. The tall man went to a cupboard containing bottles and glasses. As he brought her what she had asked for, he said, 'Considering my close association with the Androcles family, and that I'd never set eyes on you until we flew here together, I'm surprised you seem so familiar with them. What makes you think this house belongs to Andronicus Androcles?'

'Doesn't it?'

'Yes, it does. But how did you know that?'

'My lawyer told me that old Mr Cheiro Androcles had left the bulk of his property to Andronicus. I only wish it included the lien on my boat. Andronicus sounds a lot more approachable than Madame Androcles.'

'Stella has a lien on your boat? How did that come about?'

Briefly, Amalie explained. She had not intended to

confide her errand to him; it was none of his business. Perhaps the rum was making her garrulous. She put it aside, unfinished.

He looked at her thoughtfully for some moments, and then he said, 'Unlike Andronicus, who has a weakness for pretty women, Stella doesn't like her own sex—and the prettier they are the less she likes them. You are very attractive, Miss Heron. I think you would be well advised to appoint me as your intermediary. I have a good deal of influence over Madame Androcles.'

She felt like retorting, *I'm sure you have*, but she bit it back.

'I think I can almost guarantee to persuade her to restore the original terms of the loan her late husband made to your grandfather,' he went on. 'Why not leave it to me?'

Suddenly Amalie felt exhausted. She supposed it must be a reaction to the shock of her grandfather's death, the shock of the debts looming over her, the shock of being cornered by the dog.

She said limply, 'All right ... if you can. I should be eternally grateful.'

'How grateful, Miss Heron?'

As he spoke, his blue eyes roved over her slender figure in a way that made it impossible to misunderstand him.

Her cheeks burned with indignant colour.

'Not as grateful as that, I'm afraid,' she said, with a snap. 'My standards are rather different from yours.'

His smile made mock of her outrage. 'Surely to get rid of that punitive interest would be worth ... a kiss,' he said mildly.

A kind of rage rose in Amalie, a rage against people like him who devalued human relationships, and debased love as she understood it.

'I only kiss men I love,' she said, with disdain. 'If that

means that you won't help—too bad. Now, if you don't mind, I'll go home.'

'I'll take you.'

'Please don't bother—I'll bus.'

The next morning, going ashore, she was stopped by a small island boy with a note which he said was for her.

'Are you sure it's for me?'

He responded with vigorous nods.

The message was brief, and unbelievable.

Madame Androcles is happy to waive the interest imposed, in error, by her accountant. She will also be glad to supply a reliable seaman to assist you until such time as you have made other arrangements.

CHAPTER TWO

AMALIE'S first reaction was to scramble into her dinghy and scull round to *Carrageen*'s berth to share the good news with the Scotts.

Only Angela Scott was aboard.

'Goodness! How extremely enterprising,' was her comment, when Amalie had explained how she had gained admission to Paradise. 'But I don't think I should tell that part to Mr Blunt, if I were you. He might not approve of your unorthodox methods.'

'No, I'm sure he'd be shocked,' agreed Amalie. 'You aren't, are you, Lady Scott?'

'No, indeed. I'm amused—and I'm sure your grandfather would have roared. He was rather a scamp in his youth, and what you did yesterday is very much in line with some of his early escapades. Who was the man who rescued you from the dog, and then offered to intercede for you? Was he a member of the family?'

'No, no—he was the bodyguard. You remember: you mentioned him to me.'

'I see. That seems to support the gossip that he and the old man's widow are lovers. He must have great influence over her. Is he very good-looking? One sees her about a good deal, but he's never with her.'

'He's very ... male,' said Amalie. 'I shouldn't describe him as handsome. He looks rather nice—if one doesn't know anything about him.'

'I wonder why he's been so helpful? You don't think he might have it in mind to make a nuisance of himself? You're an attractive girl, and he may be bored with the widow and looking for other diversions. I should think a man of that type would be completely unscrupulous in his relations with women.'

'As a matter of fact, he did make a mild sort of pass at me. But I told him to get lost—which is why this is such a surprise,' said Amalie, brandishing the unsigned note, neatly typed on Paradise writing paper.

'Your rebuff may have whetted his appetite,' pointed out Lady Scott. 'Men are said to be hunters at heart, and nowadays when—so we're told—few girls resist their advances, a girl who is not to be had for the asking may present an interesting challenge.'

'Whatever his motives for helping, I think I should thank him—and her,' said Amalie. 'I'll go and ring up right away. Perhaps this time they'll put me through to her. If not, I can write a note and hand it in at the gate. Which reminds me, I must write to Tabitha later today. Oh, what a relief not to have to cancel our bookings!'

'Let's hope the seaman they're supplying *will* be reliable. I daresay he will. People with plenty of money don't have to tolerate inefficiency like ordinary mortals.'

This time, when Amalie dialled the Paradise number and announced that this was Miss Heron and she wanted to thank Madame Androcles for her kindness to her, the voice at the other end did not repeat the formula that his employer was not at home.

He said, 'Madame left for the airport an hour ago, miss. She's flying to Europe, and won't return for some weeks.'

'Oh ... oh, I see. In that case I'd better write to her. You could forward a letter, couldn't you?'

'Certainly, miss.'

'Thank you.' She was on the point of saying goodbye, when a thought struck her. 'They've both gone to Europe, presumably? Madame Androcles and ... the tall man?'

'The tall man, miss?' Now the voice seemed to have the same guarded note she had heard when she had called before.

'I don't know his name. I believe he used to be the late Mr Androcles' bodyguard.'

There was a slight hesitation before the voice said, 'Would you hold the line a moment, please?'

Amalie waited, wondering what was happening at the other end. Presently there was a click, and a voice she recognised said, 'Bodyguard speaking. Good morning. What can I do for you?'

He sounded amused, and she said, 'Is that an out-of-date term for your occupation? I don't know the current one.'

'Perhaps it would simplify matters if I told you my name. It's Blake.'

'Blake? B-l-a-k-e?'

'Correct.'

'But that's an English name, and I thought you told me you weren't English.'

'Half English, half Greek. The Greek side predominates.'

'Oh, I see. I rang up to thank you very much for persuading Madame Androcles to waive the interest, and also for solving my crew problem.'

'There is one condition with regard to the crew,' he told her.

'What's that?'

'That you'll have dinner with me tonight. Not here. In a restaurant in town where I can't possibly get out of line,' he added.

It was easy to picture the mocking gleam in his eyes. She said, 'And after dinner? Can I rely on your not getting out of line then?'

'You can—unless by that stage of the evening you've changed your mind.'

'I shan't change it,' she said firmly. 'Very well, Mr Blake, I will dine with you. I'd like to know something about this seaman you're supplying. What time shall we meet, and where?'

'I'll pick you up at seven-thirty. I can easily find out where you're berthed. Do you like seafood?'

'Very much.'

'So do I. That's a promising start. Until tonight, then.'

He rang off, leaving her to wonder what had possessed her to agree to meet him. She could have asked about the seaman on the telephone. Obviously Lady Scott's supposition had been well founded. He was accustomed to bowling women over like ninepins, and determined not to have his first failure with her.

But Amalie was equally determined to resist his undeniable magnetism with every ounce of her will-power, and she left the telephone booth with her chin up and a martial light in her wide-set greenish grey eyes.

During the afternoon Roderick came on board to invite her to join a water-skiing party to be followed by a beach barbecue.

'I should have loved it, but I'm afraid I'm not free,' she told him. 'I have an engagement this evening.'

He looked surprised, and she felt obliged to explain the nature of the engagement.

He had already been put in the picture by his mother, and now he said, 'Is that wise? I gather this man is an unpleasant type—what Father's generation called a blackguard.'

'He may be a blackguard, but one couldn't call him unpleasant. Being pleasant to women must be part of his stock in trade,' she said dryly. 'Don't worry about me, Roderick. I can look after myself.'

'Yes, I suppose a girl with your looks must have acquired a good deal of experience in fending men off.'

Amalie, accustomed to thinking of Tabitha as a beauty and herself as in no way outstanding, gave him a startled glance. She had not set much store by his mother's compliment, during their conversation in the morning, because she knew people of Lady Scott's age were inclined to describe as attractive girls considered non-starters among their own generation. But for Roderick to speak of 'your looks' in that tone did mean something.

'I wouldn't say that, but I certainly don't intend to become one of the scalps on Mr Blake's belt. On the other hand it would have been pretty ungracious to refuse to dine with him in a public place when he has just removed —or been instrumental in removing—such a huge weight from my shoulders.'

'I suppose it would,' he agreed. 'Pity about the barbecue. I think you'd have enjoyed it more than dinner in the kind of expensive tourist-trap where you'll probably wind up tonight.'

'I'm sure I should have, and I hope you'll ask me again some time.'

'You can be certain of that. 'Bye for the moment.'

He clambered down to his dinghy, leaving Amalie to take a shower before returning on deck to dry her hair in the sun.

Seafarer was berthed between a cutter and a brigantine, neither vessel having anyone on board them at the present time. Amalie hoped they would remain battened. It gave her an extra degree of privacy without leaving her in any way isolated from the busy life of the harbour.

As she sat in a deck-chair in the bows, with her bare feet propped on one of the rails of the pulpit, lazily brushing her hair, the only flaw in her contentment was the absence of the old man who, much more than her father, had been the exemplar of the standards by which now she judged all his sex.

When her hair was dry, she fetched a pen and a pad and wrote a long letter to Tabitha, recounting much but not all that had happened since her arrival.

She was already ashore, perched on a bollard, when in the distance she saw a tall, unmistakable figure strolling along the far end of the quay. It lacked five minutes to the time he had said he would fetch her, and he was pausing to look over some of the boats.

As he came nearer she saw that he was wearing a string-coloured silk tweed suit, the unlined jacket unbuttoned to show a darker shirt, a leather belt and the latest style of tie.

Amalie knew enough about men's clothes to recognise that, although the effect was casual, everything he wore was expensive. She wondered what he would think of her black and white dress, cinched with a wide emerald belt, which came from an Oxford Street chain store. Strappy black high-heeled sandals and a tiny cylindrical black bag on a long cord completed her outfit. She felt she looked reasonably chic, but her dress was not to be compared with the clothes by designers such as Emanuel and Genny which Stella Androcles, and women like her, wore to dine at Caribbean nightspots.

Before he reached her, she rose and walked towards him.

'Good evening,' he said, when they were within speaking range. 'I'm not late, I hope. I stopped to look at a cutter down there called *Passalimani*, after the harbour at Piraeus which, as you probably know, is the port of Athens.'

As he spoke, his blue eyes ranged slowly from her newly washed hair to her toes which, an hour ago, she had painted a pearly shell colour. She felt it was not her dress but the body inside it he was appraising.

'You're not late. I'm always early. *Passalimani* must have put in this afternoon. There wasn't a boat of that name there when I came by earlier.'

'Speaking of names,' he asked, 'what's your first name? You don't expect me to go on calling you Miss Heron, I hope?'

'My name is Amalie.'

Sometimes, when she told her name to someone who

had never heard it before, they thought she meant Emily. He didn't make that mistake. He said, 'There's a town called Charlotte Amalie, after a Danish queen, up in the United States Virgin Islands.'

'Is there? I didn't know that. I really know very little about any of the Leeward Islands. My grandfather preferred the Windwards.'

They had begun to stroll back in the direction from which he had come, and she asked, 'What is your Christian name?'

'Rather a ludicrous one, in the opinion of my English schoolfellows. Even now I prefer not to reveal it except to very close intimates, which you are not—yet,' he added, with a glinting glance. 'Therefore Blake, which is both a Christian name and a surname, is my all-purpose name.'

'I don't think I've come across it as a first name before.'

'Haven't you? It's an old Anglo-Saxon name meaning, so I've been told, "black" or "dark-complexioned". Very suitable for me, don't you think?'

'So your father was English and your mother Greek, but you say your Greek side predominates. I should have thought it would be the other way about, particularly if you were educated in England.'

'My father died when I was an infant, and my holidays, which I enjoyed much more than being at school, were spent with my Greek relations. The pleasant times of one's life count for more than the disagreeable periods, wouldn't you agree?'

'Oh, yes, I should,' she said fervently. 'My whole life has been influenced by the one marvellous year I spent out here with my grandfather when I was fourteen. I knew I'd found my place in the world, and I couldn't wait to get back to it.'

They had reached the far end of the quay. Amalie caught sight of the silver sports car, an abrupt and unpleasant reminder of his relationship with Madame Androcles.

She found that, for a few minutes, she had forgotten what manner of man Blake was, and had even experienced an uprush of sympathy for the schoolboy teased by his fellows because he bore a Greek name. Aristotle, perhaps, or Socrates.

Not that the man beside her looked as if he had ever been the kind of small, timid boy who would have been easy to bully.

He slipped a hand under her elbow and steered her towards the sleek car. 'Where did you live in England?' he asked.

'First in Hampshire and then in London.'

'Small world. My school was in Hampshire.'

'You're not an old Wykehamist, are you?'

As soon as she had asked the question, she felt it to be a foolish one. Roderick Scott might have been to Winchester, the first English public school, founded by William of Wykeham in the fourteenth century. But this man with his palm cupping her elbow was, for all his civilised manners, a different species from Roderick.

However, to her surprise, instead of saying no, he wasn't, after some hesitation, and with an air of reluctance, he said, 'Yes, I am.' And then, with a shrug and a laugh, he added, 'But as we say in Greece, *O mandis rigas ki'an yeni pali mandies mirizi*, which means, Even if a sorcerer becomes a king, he will still smell like a sorcerer, which is equivalent to the expression that one can't make a silk purse from a sow's ear. Five years at Winchester didn't succeed in transforming me into an English gentleman. I come from a line of Greek island fishermen and seamen, and I still find them more congenial than the men with whom I was at school.'

He was obviously referring to his mother's forebears, and she concluded he must be the child of a mésalliance between an Englishman of the privileged classes and

a Greek peasant girl. Perhaps he was not legitimate, although in that case it seemed unlikely that his father's
family would have felt obliged to send him to an expensive school, possibly his father's old school. More probably a marriage had taken place, the father had died not
long afterwards, and the grandparents would have liked
to take over the boy had not the mother asserted her
rights to him.

If that was the case, he must have grown up never
quite knowing where he belonged, and subject to all the
bad effects which an insecure childhood was said to have
on a person's character.

'Enough about me. I want to know more about you,'
he said, as he put her into the car.

A second surprise was that, when she mentioned her
parents' death, he asked, 'Was your father Michael
Heron, the conductor?'

'Yes. How did you guess?'

'I saw him conduct at the Proms a couple of times.
He was the natural successor to Sir Malcolm Sargent.'

'I believe so. Are you keen on music?'

'Not particularly. At that time I was interested in a
girl who was very keen on it. She used to gaze worshipfully at your father while I gazed at her.'

'Worshipfully or predatorily?' was Amalie's response,
uttered without pause to consider the wisdom of such a
remark.

'Oh, predatorily, I feel sure. Even in my salad days I
was never inclined to put women on pedestals. Like my
Greek forebears, I consider a woman's proper place is
in the kitchen or in bed.'

'And where is a man's proper place, in your opinion?
Not earning his living by honest toil, one gathers,' she
said, on a tart note.

He laughed, showing excellent teeth. 'You don't approve of bodyguarding as an occupation, it seems?'

'It depends on the body being guarded. I don't disapprove of guarding a rich old man, if he needs to be protected. But being watchdog to his wealthy widow doesn't strike me as much of a job.'

Having spoken her mind, she remembered too late that, whatever she might think of his morals, this man had done her a favour—an immense favour.

She said hurriedly, 'I'm sorry, I had no right to say that. I should be expressing my gratitude for the success of your intercession. How on earth did you manage to persuade Madame Androcles to be so magnanimous?'

'How do you think?' was his sardonic retort.

Amalie flushed. There was an awkward silence which lasted until, not far out of town, Blake swung the car off the road into the drive of what had once been a private house and now had the sign of a guest house outside the gate.

Having parked the car among several others, he switched off the engine and turned to her.

'What makes you conclude, as clearly you do, that I am Madame Androcles' lover? Some gossip you've heard, I suppose? Gossip isn't always reliable.'

For the first time in their acquaintance his eyes held no lurking twinkle, but stared at her coldly and sternly. His whole face seemed to have hardened, as if he had let fall a mask to reveal, beneath the persona of the smooth, charming, quizzical womaniser, a man of a different metal.

Under that penetrating gaze, Amalie found herself saying uncomfortably, 'I—I saw you together. I wasn't intending to spy ... just to see who was there. So I climbed the wall round the pool. Then, as it was obviously the wrong moment to try to speak to Madame Androcles, I climbed down and hid in the bushes until the dog found me.'

'And what you saw from the wall confirmed the rumours about us?' he asked, one dark eyebrow raised.

'You seemed on familiar terms. She called you sweetie,

and you called her Stella. And she took off the top of her bikini. I know lots of people do that now, at the beach, but surely not when they're alone with a man who isn't either their husband or their lover?'

A slight smile relaxed the former harsh set of his mouth, and he said, 'You have a point there. But, if you think back, you'll recall that, although we were not aware that we had an onlooker, nothing happened that couldn't have been seen by an audience of elderly spinsters. They might not have approved of Stella's gesture, but it didn't cause me to commit any grave improprieties.'

'No ... no, it didn't,' she agreed. 'Are you saying that the gossip is untrue?'

'Would it make any difference? You still wouldn't trust me, I fancy.'

'You can't blame me for that,' she retorted. 'If you wanted to be taken for a chivalrous man, you shouldn't have said what you did yesterday ... about my repaying your help,' she added, as he looked puzzled.

'Ah, yes—but how was I to know what kind of girl you were?' Blake replied. 'It's not men who have out-moded chivalry; it's women themselves, with their claims to be treated as equals. Men, meeting girls who attract them, have always thought straightaway about making love to them. Until our times they used to conceal the fact, sometimes for months. Even among our parents' generation, it wasn't usual for the so-called good girls to sleep with them until they were safely engaged or, in many cases, married. But you know as well as I do that all that has gone by the board. Your generation of women proclaim your equality with us in every sphere from sun-bathing stripped to the waist to one-night stands with men whom you happen to fancy. Having abandoned chastity and mystery, you can't reasonably expect to be treated like old-fashioned virgins,' he finished dryly.

'Not everyone has abandoned chastity,' she protested.

'Haven't they? All those I meet seem to have done so,'

he said, with a cynical curl of his wide, well-cut mouth. 'Perhaps you are the exception, but if so'—and the look which swept from her lips to her slender brown legs expressed his doubts of the premise being a sound one—'you must have uncommon powers of resistance. How old are you?'

'Twenty ... almost.'

'Almost twenty years old, with lines as pleasing to the eye as that schooner of yours, and as yet still an unplucked blossom,' he said musingly. 'That seems as unlikely as finding an untrodden beach in the Caribbean—but not impossible, perhaps.'

'And if it were so, would I then be able to trust you to behave as men used to with "good" girls?'

He considered the question for a moment. 'If it were so —yes, certainly you could. There's not much enjoyment to be found in the arms of a virgin, and a girl who was still one at twenty would be far too frigid for my taste. But I don't think you're frigid, Amalie—not with that mouth like Botticelli's Primavera.'

His gaze moved from her eyes to her lips, causing a faint tremor in her. Before she guessed his intention, he leaned towards her and put his warm mouth against hers.

It was the briefest of contacts. She had no time to recoil before he sat back in his seat, and said, 'No, of course you aren't.'

There was a hiatus: a matter of seconds in which she made a discovery which shocked and bewildered her. The man was almost a stranger, and yet she did not want to lose his interest by admitting that her experience was as narrow as his was wide.

'Come, let's go in and eat. I booked our table for eight o'clock, and Marguerite doesn't like people to be late,' he said.

The house was built on a slope overlooking the sea, and a balustraded platform, too large to be called a balcony or a veranda, had been built out from the ground floor. Here, at fewer than a dozen tables, most of them already occupied, people were dining under the lively supervision of an immensely stout woman who, so Blake said later, was the descendant of a French planter and one of his slaves.

Marguerite was a superb cook who told Amalie that, normally, she catered only for the people staying at her guest house.

'But this big *type* is a friend, and when he called by to tell me he had met a lovely girl who must have the best food on the island, I said I would make an exception.'

'Not for the first time, I imagine,' said Amalie, when Margurite had returned to the kitchen.

'No, I eat here often, but usually alone. This isn't a place where women can show themselves off. The people who stay here are mostly on a tight budget. Also Marguerite doesn't take kindly to diners smoking between the courses, or indeed at the end of the meal if other people are still eating. I knew you were a non-smoker.'

'How did you know?'

'You didn't light up on the plane, and your hair, when I had to lean near you while the pilot was dealing with the door, smelt of shampoo rather than smoke. My dislike of smoking is my one and only streak of puritanism. For all the other sensual pleasures I have nothing but enthusiasm. You don't keep that admirable shape by dieting, I hope?'

She shook her head. 'Certainly not when I'm dining out. Tell me about this seaman you've rustled up for me. Is he a local man? When can he start?'

'You don't need him until your first charter party arrive on the scene, do you?'

'No, not really. I can manage the advance preparations —loading the stores and so on—by myself.'

'On what date do they turn up?' Blake asked. When

she had told him, he said, 'Then I suggest that your man reports for duty the day before. Until then he's more usefully occupied elsewhere. You needn't worry about his capabilities. He'll be able to do anything you ask of him, except in the galley. He won't be much help with the catering.'

'That doesn't matter. That's my pidgin. It's something I'm looking forward to. I'm hoping to build up a reputation for providing the finest food on any boat in these waters.'

'You should get together with Marguerite,' he told her. 'She knows all there is to know about the dishes peculiar to the Caribbean. I think she might be able to give you some useful advice.'

'I'm sure she could,' agreed Amalie.

Certainly the meal which they enjoyed that night was as good as anything to be had in the various restaurants in London where she had been taken by the men she had dated. They began with Trinidadian pastelles of seasoned minced meat wrapped in banana leaves. The main course was soft-shell crabs, crisply fried in breadcrumbs and served with a sharp-tasting rémoulade sauce and a green salad. The wine was as good as the food, and every detail of the presentation was satisfying: the plain white, piping hot plates, the French-style paper cloth over the undercloth, the large check cotton napkins, the good butter and hot crusty rolls, and the grinders for black peppercorns and sea salt should the diners wish to augment Marguerite's seasoning.

After the cheeses came fresh pineapple, and then coffee with which, without consulting his companion, Blake asked for something called Williamine.

'Have you had this before?' he enquired, when Marguerite's assistant brought two liqueur glasses and filled them with a pale distilled spirit.

When Amalie shook her head, he said, 'It's a favourite

of mine—made from pears. It follows well after pine-apple.'

Knowing how potent were all white liqueurs she sipped it with a certain caution and had to agree the flavour was particularly delicious.

As a trained cook herself, she had liked the appreciative relish with which Blake had eaten his dinner. She had wondered beforehand if he might try to ply her with wine, but although he had once or twice added a little to her glass while refilling his own, he had not seemed to notice how slowly she had been drinking, or urged her to speed up her consumption.

'If you don't mind, I'd rather not be too late getting back, I'm an early riser, and I need my eight hours,' she said, after a second cup of coffee.

They had been talking about music. In spite of his earlier disclaimer, it was clear that Blake was more than ordinarily informed on the subject of opera and orchestral music. Amalie, too, in spite of her parents' disappointment with her lack of performing talent, inevitably had picked up a great deal of knowledge, particularly in relation to Tabitha's instrument, the cello.

However, saying goodbye to Marguerite, and arranging for Amalie to call on her, brought an end to this safe conversation and, taking her seat in the car while Blake held the door, she could think of no way to resume it.

'Aren't you nervous, sleeping alone on the boat?' he asked, as they drove out of the gateway.

'No, not at all. I bolt the main hatch and feel as safe as in London. The Scotts did mention that burglaries from boats had increased in the last year or two, but that's mostly during the daytime when boats are left unattended. People don't break in during the night much.'

'Who are the Scotts?'

'A mother and son, also in the charter business, who were very friendly with Grandpa.'

'What's the son like?' he asked.

'Roderick? He seems very nice.'

'How old?'

'I'm not sure. Early twenties. A year or two older than I am.'

'But not interested in girls, perhaps?'

'It isn't that sort of mother-and-son relationship. His father, a retired admiral, was alive until fairly recently, and Roderick has taken over from him. He and his mother are obviously very fond of each other, but not obsessively devoted.'

'Perhaps he'll become fond of you,' commented Blake.

'Anything is possible. I shouldn't think it at all likely.'

'In other words, he hasn't made much impact on you.'

'I didn't say that. He seems to be extremely pleasant. But I've only just met the man. I really know nothing about him.'

'You've only just met me,' said Blake. 'But don't tell me you haven't thought that it might be pleasant, to-night, not to sleep on your own for a change.'

Amalie's whole posture stiffened, and she said, in an indignant tone, 'I haven't thought any such thing! If you want to know what I *have* been thinking, it's that I hope you don't mean to spoil an otherwise pleasant evening by ... by overstepping the mark when we say goodnight.'

Blake put back his dark head and laughed. 'And just where is the mark, Mis' Amalie honey?—repeating the form of address used by Marguerite in saying goodnight.

She remembered his mouth touching hers and knew that, if she were honest, she would like him to do it again but a little more lingeringly. But she knew he wasn't the type to go in for gentle goodnights.

Aloud she said, '*I* should prefer to shake hands.'

'Little liar,' was his good-humoured comment. And then, 'Well, we'll see when we get there'—a remark which effectively prevented her from relaxing again for the rest of the drive.

It was a beautiful night, as indeed all nights were at

this latitude and at this season. But Amalie had been in the Caribbean for too short a time to take the warm moonlight for granted.

The water in the harbour shimmered like cloth of silver, and the masts of the boats resembled an unearthly silver forest filled with the soft, tinkling music of shrouds and stays strummed by the trade wind. It was this refreshing wind which saved the West Indian nights from being uncomfortably humid.

Because it was earlier than most people ended an evening out, many of the moored vessels had people sitting in the cockpits or on the decks.

Their presence reassured Amalie. Blake could not force his way on board *Seafarer*, and she thought it unlikely that he would attempt an embrace on the quay where there would be witnesses if she rebuffed him.

When they came near to *Seafarer*, he said, 'Which is your dinghy?'

She pointed it out, and he bent to untie the painter for her.

Amalie slipped off her sandals and, as she did so, said in a tone of, she hoped, composed politeness, 'I won't ask you aboard for a nightcap, but thank you very much for a most enjoyable dinner, and for introducing me to Marguerite.'

'My pleasure,' was his reply, as he towed the dinghy along to the nearest flight of steps. 'Allow me to hand you aboard,' he added, preceding her down them.

Oh dear! When she stepped inboard was he going to try to follow? she wondered, quailing at the thought.

But on the landing stage he transferred the painter from his right hand to his left in order to shake hands with her.

'Since this is the way you prefer,' he murmured, mocking her. His handclasp was strong, and she felt her knuckles crunch slightly under the pressure of his grip.

'Goodnight, Blake.' She stepped aboard, dropped her

bag and her sandals, and sat down on the wooden thwart.

'Goodnight.' He let go of the painter, tossing it inboard and nudging the dinghy away from the steps with his foot.

As she dipped the paddle in the water, he did not return up the steps but stood with his hands in his pockets, watching her, smiling faintly.

Clearly he was not seriously put out by her refusal to let him stay the night with her. Presumably he thought she was playing hard to get, and he was prepared to bide his time. She could tell that he hadn't a doubt that she found him attractive. Of that he seemed totally confident —and, of course, he was right.

Had there been others before him, and had her values been different, perhaps she would have let him stay, and enjoyed great pleasure in his arms.

Half way to the schooner, suddenly she remembered the letter to Stella Androcles which she had meant to give to him earlier, but had forgotten and left on board.

'Blake ... don't go!' she called, seeing him turn to go up the stairs. She reversed her strokes, returning the way she had come.

'Changed your mind?' he asked, waiting for her.

'No, no ... it's not that.' She blushed. 'I—I wrote a note to Madame Androcles and forgot to give it to you to be forwarded to her in London. Would you mind waiting while I fetch it?'

'Not at all.'

Regardless of possible damage to his light-coloured trousers, he sat down on the steps to wait for her.

Slightly hampered by her full skirt, Amalie climbed on board the schooner, fetched the letter from the saloon, and hastened over the side again.

As she came near him, Blake said, 'I'll do better than forward it. I can deliver it by hand. I'm going to London myself on the morning plane.'

'Oh ... are you? For long?'

'I don't know. Perhaps. Shall I leave a gap in your life?'

Ignoring the teasing question, she held out the letter and said, 'Well ... bon voyage, and thank you again for your help.'

He had seemed so relaxed, sitting there with one long leg bent and the other outstretched. Amalie wouldn't have believed that anyone lounging as he had been could spring into action as swiftly. Before she knew what was happening he had not only seized the painter, but scooped her out of the dinghy and into his arms.

She gasped, too startled to struggle.

He put his lips to her cheek and said, in a low, husky voice, '*Had we but world enough and time, this coyness, lady, were no crime.* But you're beautiful, Amalie, and I want you—tonight.'

Several men had kissed her, but none with the bold assurance with which Blake stifled her protest and took possession of her lips. This was nothing at all like the kiss he had given her earlier. That had been a kiss for a girl, and this was a kiss for a woman; a long, sensuous, passionate kiss which seemed to sweep over her with the force of a hurricane.

She emerged from it panting and trembling: part of her rigid with rage at his violation of her wishes, and part of her stirred to the point when she would have been forced to respond had he not raised his head.

Her face was in full moonlight as he held her against him and looked down into her eyes. Whatever he saw there made him frown, and say harshly, 'My God! I didn't believe it, but you are a virgin.' He let her go and stepped away, the painter still coiled round his knuckles and the dinghy secure.

'Y-you make it sound like a crime,' she retorted angrily.

How could he be sure from one kiss? His slighting tone made her feel as if, for him, kissing her had been like flat beer or cold porridge. Yet for her it had been an emotional cataclysm.

'Not a crime. A considerable surprise—and a disappointment. I have very few scruples, but I do draw the line at seducing naïve girls who don't know the ropes. Not that I've met one before,' he added dryly.

'Perhaps you move in the wrong circles. May I please have the painter?' Humiliation made her voice shake.

As he unwound the rope from his hand, she snatched it from him and would have stepped blindly into the dinghy had he not restrained her.

'Steady on! You don't want a ducking.'

She flung off his hand, but stepped inboard more carefully. Without another glance at him she paddled hurriedly back to *Seafarer*, scrambled on board, made fast the dinghy and went below.

In the saloon she flopped on the banquette, her fists clenched with impotent fury. How dared he force a kiss on her, and then deride her for not being eagerly responsive! All the other men who had kissed her had not seemed to find her wanting—although admittedly her relationships with them had never been more than mild and ephemeral romances.

She had never been deeply in love; and had no wish to experience the fever of passion except for a man she did love. She had seen other girls made unhappy by ill-judged affairs with no substance under the superficial magic of physical attraction. She did not, if she could prevent it, mean to fall into that kind of error. Yet, since the first day on the plane, when he had held her hand, she had felt Blake's power to attract her. Now, after to-night, she hoped she would never see him again.

I dislike and despise him, she told herself. He holds women cheap, as if we were no more than playthings. I'm glad he's leaving tomorrow. Let's hope he doesn't come back.

*

Roderick, with whom in the next few days she spent a good deal of her time, was a comfortable companion with whom she could safely relax. And it wasn't, as Blake had implied, because he was unattractive. He was well-built, personable, sometimes witty. But she wasn't constantly aware that he was male and she was female, as she had been with the other man. For the moment they were two people with a great many common interests, and not dissimilar backgrounds.

That their friendship might some day develop was always a possibility between any young man and woman, but it wasn't something to think about yet. For the present, they both had more pressing matters on their minds.

There was now only one week to go before Roderick went to the airport to pick up his first charter party.

'It's a two-week booking, this one, so we shan't see you again until you come back to base at the end of your one-week charter. I must say I'd feel a lot happier about leaving you on your own if I'd seen the crew you're being sent.'

'I shall be all right. Don't worry about me, Roderick.'

'You certainly seem to have remembered an amazing amount of what you learned in that one year out here, five years ago.'

As he spoke, they were leaving harbour in *Carrageen*'s fibreglass tender to have a picnic lunch and spend the afternoon swimming from a beach along the coast, Roderick's mother was not with them. She was having lunch with a friend who lived on the island.

However, before setting out for a few hours of relaxation, he had spent time making sure that Amalie knew all a charter skipper had to know before taking responsibility for the safety and comfort of six guests.

He had tested her grasp of the use of the single-side-band ship-to-shore radio, and made sure she knew by heart the two international distress frequencies, and the correct distress and urgency procedure. *Seafarer* also carried a VHF radio which would enable an aircraft to pick up a signal from her. Aboard *Carrageen*, Roderick had installed a wide-ranging 'ham' radio.

He had made sure she understood the safety precautions to be taken with the butane gas cooker, and that she knew how to operate the pump which, when the schooner was at sea, would empty the tank in the bilges which contained the waste from the heads.

These, and a dozen other tests of her proficiency, had taken up most of the morning, and although she had felt that she did know all that was necessary, the fact that he had passed her with full marks was an added boost to her confidence.

'All you need now is experience—as I still do myself,' he remarked, while they were having lunch.

They had beached the tender at a spot where for half a mile in either direction there was no one else to be seen. Amalie had provided the food—crisp round rolls with the crumb removed and replaced with smoked fish and salad —and Roderick had brought the drinks, cans of beer for himself and, knowing that she did not like beer, a large bottle of aerated water for Amalie. Before filling her glass he put in a dash of angostura bitters which made the water the colour of a pink tourmaline, and gave it a flavour something like ginger ale.

'Pink gin was the greatest wardroom drink when my father was first in the Navy,' he told her. 'Mother has a trick with angostura which she picked up from the barman at an hotel—the Berkeley, I think it was—where they used to stay. She warms a dry ice tray, sprinkles in a little angostura, and sets it alight. I suspect that part is unnecessary, but it makes the ice cubes more interesting.'

'I must try it,' said Amalie.

The tip reminded her that the following morning she was going to visit Marguerite, and with that came the thought of the man whom she was trying, not very successfully, to put out of her mind.

'You look troubled,' said Roderick. 'What's on your mind? Your sister? Perhaps you'll hear from her soon.'

'I hope so. Although somehow I can't see Tabitha exchanging letters as regularly as Grandpa and I did. But we had all the same interests. In some ways Tabby and I are more like distant cousins than sisters.'

'I don't know any musicians or other kinds of artistic people, but I should have thought they didn't need close family relationships, or even friendships, in the way that most people do. Their art fills their lives, presumably?'

'Yes, I think that's probably true—and certainly of the great ones, which Tabby may be one day.'

'When will she make her début?'

'Oh, not for some time yet, which is just as well if I'm going to be able to afford to be there.'

Their talk turned to a discussion of running expenses, harbour levies and all the financial aspects of chartering.

Later they swam and snorkeled together. Roderick stayed in the clear sea longer than Amalie, who wanted to spend half an hour improving her tan. By judicious sunbathing and the use of a high protection factor cream she had managed to brown without burning, and was now a light honey colour and no longer in any danger of reddening or peeling. But she meant to continue to use sun cream lavishly, particularly on her face, for she did not want her new life to result in premature wrinkles, and Angela Scott had bemoaned her own inadequate precautions in the days before it was realised that too much sun could be harmful rather than beneficial.

While Roderick was still in the water she undid the clip of her bra and lay face-down with her head turned sideways to watch the lovely perspective of the pale pink beach, wide where she was lying but seemingly

narrow in the distance, the pellucid pale green water—
like gin tinged with *crème de menthe*—and the wind-
curved trunks of the palm trees.

Presently, reaching behind her to re-fasten the clip before rolling on to her back, she remembered Blake's remark about topless sunbathing and the abandonment of
mystery. Try as she would to forget him, she found
thoughts of him were apt to pop into her mind at least
a dozen times a day. Where was he now? Squiring Stella
Androcles about London?

'Amalie?'

She opened her eyes. She had not heard Roderick returning.

'I thought you might be asleep. You were lying very
still.'

'No, I was only soaking up this heavenly sun.' She sat
up and started to talk to him, shutting out the disturbing memory of being pinioned, helpless, in Blake's strong
arms.

The morning with Marguerite was both useful and amusing. Among other things Amalie learnt how to make delicious pre-dinner mouthfuls by frying thin slices of
green banana or coconut meat, and she laughed at Marguerite's tales of some of her guests' eccentricities.

Blake's name did not crop up until the end of the
visit when Marguerite said, 'I thought maybe you don't
like my cooking as Blake ain't brought you here again.'

'I loved your cooking—every mouthful,' Amalie assured her. 'Blake has gone. As far as I know he's in
London with Madame Androcles.'

'You missin' him?'

Amalie raised her eyebrows as if the question surprised
her. 'No. Why should I? We only met two or three
times. It was just a holiday acquaintance.'

'That's good. That's fine,' said Marguerite.

But she did not explain what she meant by this cryptic

comment, and Amalie felt that to ask her would show too much interest in Blake.

Although she did miss the Scotts when their ketch had sailed out of the harbour, the week between *Carrageen*'s departure and the arrival of her own party were not lonely days for Amalie.

Her circle of acquaintance grew wider all the time. Many people seemed to have heard about *Seafarer*'s youthful new skipper, and went out of their way to be friendly to her.

Some of her time was spent reading her grandfather's log books; one a brief record of the schooner's course when at sea, the weather, and similar details. The second log was more in the nature of a diary, with descriptions of his charter guests, ideas for improvement to *Seafarer*, and even notes about Amalie. Some of these—showing clearly his love for her—brought tears to her eyes as she read them.

She knew that for her perfect happiness would arrive when she found a man who, in character, humour and kindness, bore a close resemblance to John Lawrence, and who either owned his boat or was willing to take over hers.

As the week passed, her one niggling worry was how she was going to manage if the crew promised by Madame Androcles failed to turn up. She knew from her grandfather's private log that some of his regular charterers were themselves experienced yachtsmen who enjoyed taking turns at the helm. But this did not apply to her first party who although, according to his records, had been recommended by regulars, were all first-timers. They were a young married couple with their parents and parents-in-law. Perhaps they knew about sailing, and perhaps they didn't. Either way, they were expecting *Seafarer* to be a crewed boat on which they were not obliged to exert themselves in any way unless they volunteered to do so.

The morning before their arrival Amalie set out for the market with a fervent prayer in her heart that, by night-fall, she would have her crew.

At the market she met a girl with whom she had become friendly. She was one of the crew of a headboat, a large Baltic trader catering to upwards of a dozen individual passengers rather than the kind of small family party Amalie was expecting.

She and Lynn had a milk shake together, and the sun was high and very hot as, her basket laden with melons, bananas and paw-paws, she made her way back to the harbour.

At first sight, the graceful white schooner looked exactly as she had left her. But when Amalie mounted the boarding ladder and heaved her load inboard, she saw something which made her heart leap with relief.

Propped against the main hatch, which was locked, was a serviceable blue canvas duffel bag. Attached to the bag was a note. *Back at 1700.*

Several times during the afternoon she re-examined the message in the hope of deriving some clue as to what kind of man she was going to have living on board with her.

But the note, which was written on one of the Memorandum pages torn from the back of a pocket diary, did not give much away. The writing was small and neat, the stem of the 7 being crossed in the Continental fashion. It was not the hand of a seaman with very little schooling, but other than that it told her nothing.

For half an hour before five she sat under *Seafarer*'s awning, idly turning the pages of one of her grandfather's books of poetry, and waiting to hear herself hailed.

Now and then, when a line caught her eye, she would pause to read the whole verse. But most of the time she was watching to see a stranger approaching, and have a quick preview of her crew.

> *For I,*
> *Except you enthrall me, never shall be free,*
> *Nor ever chaste, except you ravish me.*

Her glance flickered down the page to the name of the poet. John Donne, the seventeenth-century preacher, and most erotic of English poets, from whose lines the American novelist Ernest Hemingway had taken his famous title, *For Whom The Bell Tolls.*

She had read Donne before, at school, but never this poem, these lines. They touched a chord deep inside her. She read them again. Clearly, in this context *except* must be read as *unless. For I, Unless you enthrall me*——

'Ahoy, *Seafarer*!'

Momentarily gripped by the poem, her response to the voice hailing her was automatic rather than conscious. She lifted blank eyes from the page, and stared for a moment or two at the man on the quay.

He was wearing blue jeans, and his shirt was slung over his shoulder, leaving bare a strong, sunburned chest. His forehead and eyes were shaded by the peak of a helmsman's white cap; not a new one such as those worn by some of the tourists, but a shabby old cap like the one John Lawrence had worn.

Amalie put down the book and stood up.

'What do you want?' she called to him.

'To come aboard,' he called back. A grin creased Blake's gypsy-dark cheeks. 'I'm your new crew, Miss Heron . . . Skipper.'

CHAPTER THREE

SHOCK and dismay—mixed with another reaction which she did not recognise until later—held her frozen for fully ten seconds.

'You can't be!' she murmured aloud, but too low for her words to reach him.

Her consternation making her slower than usual, she climbed down into the dinghy and paddled to where he was waiting. But a few feet short of the landing steps, she used the paddle to break the dinghy's momentum and hold it a yard out of reach.

'I don't understand you,' she said. 'Where's the man who was going to crew for me?'

'He can't come. I'm here in his place. Don't worry, I'm a perfectly competent substitute. As I told you, I come from a long line of seafaring men.'

'But I don't want you,' she said bluntly. 'Why can't the other man come?'

'Because his old father is ill, probably dying, and the Androcles family are not so heartless as to send him away from his island at such a time. I'm not indispensable at present, so it's better that I take his place. You may not like the idea, but I'm afraid you'll have to make the best of it.'

'Oh, will I indeed?' she said tersely. 'I'm not so sure about that!'

'My dear girl, you have no choice. Tomorrow your people arrive. If you haven't found a crew by now, it's not very likely you will at this eleventh hour.'

'I haven't been looking for one since Madame Androcles said that she could provide one. But if I'd known this might happen——'

'What are you afraid of? That I've engineered this situation with evil designs on your virtue? Don't be foolish, Amalie. I'm here because Adelpho isn't available at present. If it will ease your mind, I'll sleep ashore tonight. Tomorrow you'll have the protection of your charter party. Now let me aboard like a good girl. I want to unpack and stow my kit.'

Reluctantly, knowing he was right and she had no choice, Amalie brought the dinghy alongside the landing stage. Blake stepped lightly aboard and took over the paddle.

'I haven't eaten today yet. Can you fix me a meal, or shall I find one ashore?'

'I can give you supper, or you can have a cooked high tea straight away if you wish.'

'Yes, that would suit me very well. Then I'll take myself off and reappear tomorrow morning.'

On board the schooner, she said, 'I'll show you your cabin. I'm afraid you'll find it rather cramped after living in luxury at Paradise.'

'I expect I'll adjust.'

She led him below, showed him the heads and the shower, and then passed on to his quarters close to the bows.

'This is fine,' said Blake, putting down his duffel bag and glancing round the small but not ill-equipped cabin which was to be his.

'You'll find a wind scoop in the hanging cupboard, and in here'—she opened a locker—'there's a small net hammock which fixes on those two hooks if you need extra stowage. Now I'll go and cook something for you. It will take about half an hour, so you've time for a shower if you'd like one.'

'Thank you, I should,' he replied. 'How much water do you carry?'

'Three hundred gallons, which is plenty for a week's

cruise if it isn't wasted, and Grandpa made sure of that by fitting spring-loaded taps. There's no need to stint on showers. They use very little.' She left him to unpack his bag.

Seafarer was equipped with a freezer as well as a refrigerator, and also had two large cool boxes for block ice on deck so that anyone wanting a cold drink did not have to come below. Amalie had already thawed out two beefsteaks for her own and the new crew's supper, and a salad, prepared that morning, was in the crisper of the fridge, needing only to be tossed in French dressing.

While she peeled potatoes for *pommes frites,* and rinsed the strips in cold water to take off the starch, she pondered the truth of Blake's statement that he had no ulterior motive for taking the place of the man called Adelpho.

It was true, as he had pointed out, that once the charterers arrived, he would have little opportunity to make any passes at her. But between each charter came the turn-round, for which her grandfather always allowed a minimum of forty-eight hours and sometimes longer.

Unless she insisted on Blake staying ashore at those times, and paid for his accommodation, there would be two days and nights when they would be alone on the schooner between each cruise.

Having dried the *frites* with kitchen paper, she gave them their first deep-fat frying to soften them. They could then be set on one side to await the last-moment frying which would brown and crisp them.

As she did this, she remembered her chagrin at being told that, because she was a virgin, she was of no interest to him. At the same time she had not forgotten that, shortly before he had made that mortifying statement, he had told her she was beautiful, and murmured, *I want you, Amalie.*

What if, as the season progressed, and there were no

other women with whom he could amuse himself, his vaunted scruples gave place to a perverse desire to overcome her resistance?

What I'm really afraid of, she thought, is that I might not resist him.

For she knew now that what she had felt on seeing him there on the quay had been only partly dismay. Beneath her alarm and apprehension had run an undercurrent of excitement.

He had come back, and all at once she had felt alive in a way she had not felt since his departure. He was not a nice man, like Roderick, but he gave life a spice it lacked when he wasn't around.

By the time he was ready to eat, she had laid a place at the large table in the saloon which, gimballed and heavily weighted, gave a stable surface for meals even in a strong swell.

For a starter, she gave him potted shrimps. By the time he had eaten them his steak had been grilled and was flanked by two fried eggs, tomatoes and mushrooms, and a generous helping of *frites*.

'Cheese and biscuits? Fresh fruit?' she asked, when Blake put his knife and fork together.

He touched his lips with his napkin and shook his head. 'Nothing more, thanks. If that was a sample of your catering, your guests will be splendidly fed. The chips were particularly good.'

'Thank you. Black or white coffee?'

'Black, please. No, wait a minute'—as, carrying his empty plate, she turned to go back to the galley. 'Some time before they arrive, I ought to familiarise myself with where everything is kept. Just in case, in some kind of emergency, I needed to find a particular item. Do you keep any kind of stowage plan? Or could we, before I go ashore, do a tour of the lockers?'

Not knowing until she spoke that she had arrived at a decision, Amalie said. 'That won't be necessary—for you to go ashore, I mean.' She looked him straight in the eyes, and added coolly, 'I have a strong bolt inside the door of my cabin.'

Blake smiled at her, blue eyes glinting. 'You would be quite safe if you hadn't. I've never found it necessary to force my attention on unwilling women.'

When Amalie unlocked her door the following morning her nose was immediately assailed by the scent of freshly-ground coffee and toast.

She found Blake in the galley, having his breakfast standing up.

'What would you like for breakfast, Skipper? I'm no Cordon Bleu, but I can manage bacon and eggs or an omelette.'

'I have only fruit for breakfast,' she said. 'Paw-paw usually.'

Aware of him watching her, she cut through the dark golden skin of one of the smaller fruit, exposing the apricot flesh and the centre, filled with black seeds. According to Marguerite, the skin of the paw-paw could be wrapped around meat to tenderise it.

Blake poured a cup of coffee for her and, when she said she was going to drink it on deck, asked, 'Mind if I join you?'

'Not at all. I hope you found your bunk long enough for you, and the mattress comfortable?'

'The bunk is fine, thanks.'

She expected him to give her one of his mocking looks and enquire if she had slept soundly. But he didn't, and all that morning, until it was time for her to go to the airport while he went to the ice-house to fetch the blocks for the deck boxes, his manner was unfailingly business-like.

He had left the door of his cabin hooked back and, passing by, she glanced in and saw that none of his belongings was visible. Everything had been stowed away,

the bunk cover neatly replaced and the cabin left looking as if it were still unoccupied.

The charter party came in on a larger aircraft than
that which had brought Amalie to the island. To her
relief they were not overburdened with luggage as the
stowage of more than one large suitcase per person could
be something of a problem.

The dominant personality among them seemed to be
Bob Harvey, the father of the young woman. His wife
was Mary, his daughter was now Liza Webster, married
to Patrick, and Patrick's parents were Joan and Freddie.

Having engaged a second taxi at the airport, Amalie
suggested that she and the Harveys should travel in one,
and the other four in the other.

On the way to the harbour she explained that, since
they had booked their week's cruise eight months ago,
the then captain of *Seafarer* had died, but otherwise the
terms of the charter contract were unchanged.

'We're sorry to hear that. We're told he was a very
nice man, and a very experienced sailor,' said Mr Harvey.
'Who has taken over from him?'

'I have. I'm his granddaughter.'

'I see.' Clearly this information disturbed him. 'Aren't
you rather young to be in charge of a large boat? Were
you working with your grandfather before he died?'

'I had a year at sea with him,' she answered, not wanting to mislead them, but also not wanting them to start
the cruise with misgivings. 'And I'm not single-handed. I
have an excellent mate,' she added, hoping this boast
would prove true.

As soon as they set eyes on Blake, the Harvey's doubts
seemed allayed, if not altogether dispelled.

'I thought you would like to unpack and have some
lunch before we leave harbour,' she told them, when
they were all on board. 'Then we'll sail to our first night's
anchorage, which shouldn't take more than two hours,
and there you can swim and snorkel, or just relax.'

'Perhaps you'd like to have a drink while I bring your luggage aboard and take it below for you,' suggested Blake.

Their suitcases were still on the quay.

'A cold drink would be very welcome,' said Mrs Webster, moving to one of the deck-chairs under the awning. She was a plump, bosomy woman wearing a synthetic dress, probably chosen for its creaselessness, but unsuitable for the heat of the Caribbean.

'I'll attend to it. You stay and chat,' murmured Blake, when Amalie would have followed him below.

He reappeared almost at once with a tray of wine glasses. Then, to her surprise, having opened one of the deck boxes, he took out a bottle of champagne. He eased off the cork, filled the six glasses, and handed them first to the women and then to the men.

'No bubbly for you two?' asked Patrick.

'We don't drink until the sun is under the yard-arm,' was Blake's smiling answer. 'Excuse me while I fetch your bags.' He swung himself over the side.

'I think a toast is called for. What shall it be? How about "To fair weather and a following wind"?' suggested Freddie.

They all repeated the toast. Having tasted the champagne, Bob Harvey looked at the label on the empty bottle. 'Ah, I thought so—the genuine article, not one of the sparkling wines which masquerade as champagne. Nothing but the best on board *Seafarer*, eh, Miss Heron?'

'That's our aim—yes,' she agreed. 'But we only launch the cruise on champagne.' Where had it come from, and how much had it cost? 'It's wine and spirits, or beer, for the rest of the trip.'

'On an "all found" cruise such as this, with drinks included, you wouldn't make much of a profit if the booze included bubbly,' said Freddie, chortling. He seemed to be a carefree type who wouldn't have worried if she had been single-handed.

'No, we shouldn't, should we?' she agreed. 'Please call us Amalie and Blake, and we'll use your first names, if we may? It's the usual thing.'

Before they had drained their glasses, Blake had dealt with their luggage and re-clipped the pelican hooks which fastened the opening in the lifelines above the bording ladder which was usually left undone in harbour.

After Amalie had shown them to the three double cabins, and told them lunch would be ready in thirty minutes, she went to find Blake. He was in the galley washing up the wine glasses.

She closed the sliding door. 'Where did the champagne come from?'

'I thought it might help to give your first cruise a good send-off.'

'It did, but what did it cost?'

'Don't worry about that. It's on me.'

'It's very good of you. Thank you.' A thought struck her. 'You haven't been out to Paradise, have you? It wasn't a bottle from their cellars?'

'Yes, it was as a matter of fact. I went to pick up a couple of books I left there.'

'Oh, Blake, you shouldn't have helped yourself to their champagne for these people.'

'They won't miss a couple of bottles out of several hundred. The butler helps himself freely. It's one of his perks.'

'So it may be, but that's no reason for you to follow his example. It's stealing,' she told him bluntly.

Her outspokenness did not seem to embarrass or annoy him. If anything, he seemed amused. 'I should have realised you might be suspicious. I can see I'll have to be more careful in future.'

'Yes, you will—and please don't open the other bottle you pinched. It can go back where it came from during the turn-round.'

'Aye, aye, Skipper.'

'It isn't funy, Blake,' she snapped. 'I know lots of people take things which belong to their employers, and don't consider themselves dishonest. But I do, and you can think me a prig if you like.'

'I don't. It's the reaction I should have expected from you if I'd stopped to consider the matter. Actually I brought the champagne for our private consumption at the end of the day when the others are turning in, and we're washing up. There's nothing like bubbly to lighten the chores. However, when I noticed the Harveys looking a bit unhappy, and you with a slightly strained air, it seemed a good plan to share the uplift.'

'They were worried when I told them about Grandpa. I think next time you'd better meet the plane, and I'll do the ice run. In this sort of situation people have more confidence in a man than in a girl.'

'I shouldn't let it ruffle you,' he said. 'The world is full of people who haven't yet accepted the gospel of the women's libbers.'

'I'm not a disciple myself. In their place, I should have more confidence in you than in me. Why did you admit to taking the champagne? You could have lied and said you'd bought it.'

'Would you have believed me?'

'Probably.'

He shrugged. 'I've never been much of a liar—except for the lies we all tell to spare people's feelings.'

'You don't count a lie as white if it saves your own face?'

He polished the last of the glasses. 'Your opinion of me was already low before I admitted to taking Androcles' champagne,' was his negligent answer. 'But whatever you think of me, you're stuck with me for the time being, and I'll try not to err again.'

'That reminds me,' she said, 'we haven't discussed your pay, or how long you can go on crewing for me.'

'No, but we haven't time now. You promised them lunch in half an hour,' he reminded her.

Remembering her grandfather's comment in one of his letters that, although he would enjoy more adventurous food when they were on their own together, the charterers tended to prefer plain, familiar food, Amalie had chosen cold chicken for the first lunch of the cruise. She had even abstained from rubbing the salad bowl with garlic in case they disliked the flavour.

As a starter she gave them country pâté with hot toast and, for pudding, a fresh fruit salad, with plenty of kirsch sprinkled on it, and whipped cream handed round separately. The men had biscuits and cheese, but the women proclaimed themselves unable to eat another morsel.

All six had changed out of their travelling clothes and were now in shorts—Mrs Webster in a cotton skirt—light shirts, and sun-tops. Foreseeing that, pale as they were, they could spend their first night at sea with sore shoulders and thighs if they didn't take care, Amalie said, 'If you don't mind my making a suggestion, I think it would be advisable to plaster on plenty of sun cream before we get under way. The awning has to come down, and it's easy to burn out at sea. Perhaps you'd like to do that now while Blake and I are clearing the decks,' she suggested. 'Have you brought cream with you? If not, there's plenty on board.'

Seafarer left the harbour under the power of her diesel engine, and they did not set sail until they were in open water.

By the time they were on the wind it was clear that Blake knew precisely what he was about, and did whatever was necessary with the same unhurried expertise as her grandfather.

Amalie took the first trick at the wheel. She had already been out of harbour with Roderick, and recaptured the thrill of feeling the helm come alive under her hands.

When he had nothing to do, Blake made himself pleasant to the passengers. But all the time he was alert, and needed no warning shout that she was putting the helm down to go about.

When Patrick came to talk to her, she asked him if he would like to take a turn, and soon established that he and his father had both done a good deal of sailing. This, no doubt, was why they had seemed less concerned by the change of skipper than Bob Harvey.

Amalie had charted the cruise with advice from the Scotts and, as luck would have it, they found the crescent-shaped bay which was their first night-stop empty of any other vessel. Perhaps it might not remain deserted all evening, but when they arrived and came to anchor, it was all theirs and as idyllically lovely as a photograph in a brochure.

It wasn't long before five of the party were in the sea, but Mrs Webster, although she could swim, was nervous out of her depth, so Blake offered to row her ashore to bathe in the shallows.

Much as she would have liked to join the swimmers, Amalie stayed on deck to check the prowess of the others. She would take it more lightly in time, perhaps, but for the present she was intensely conscious of her responsibility for them. Whatever went wrong on this cruise—she hoped nothing would—it would be her fault for not foreseeing every hazard.

Presently, when it was clear that the five splashing happily about in the sunlit water were all good to very good swimmers, she turned her attention to Mrs Webster. Blake was still with her, half floating, half swimming backwards, and keeping a little ahead of Mrs Webster's jerky breast-stroke. She was wearing a pink petalled cap to protect her hair, but still keeping her head and shoulders well out of the water in the manner of people not fully at ease in that element.

She and Blake were conversing. The sound of their

voices, hers quick and light and his much deeper and
lazier, carried across the flat calm of the sheltered surface
in the bay, although the words were not audible.

Amalie thought that in terms of outlook and life-style
they could scarcely be more different; she a respectable,
middle-aged matron with a well-to-do English background which probably embraced monthly meetings of a
ladies' luncheon club, accounts at the best local stores
or shopping at Harrods when in London; and he a well-
educated but aimless hanger-on with the jet set, a mixture
of two nationalities, and with morals which would shock
his sedate companion if she ever discovered his attitude
to women and other people's property.

So it made her smile inwardly when, later, Joan Webster came to look round the galley while Amalie was
cooking the dinner.

'What a very kind, charming young man Blake is. He
was so good-humoured about taking me swimming from
the beach. I'm sure it must have bored him, keeping me
company, especially when he's such a fine swimmer himself,' she remarked.

'I'm sure it didn't bore him at all,' Amalie said diplo-
matically. 'That's what we're here for—to give you a
memorable holiday, and enjoy ourselves at the same
time.'

But privately she wondered if Blake would soon become bored, and then would leaven the monotony by
flirting with Liza Webster, who was not particularly
pretty but had a very shapely figure. He might even opt
out of crewing. He was not on a contract. There was
nothing she could do to keep him if he chose not to
stay.

For dinner she gave them consommé, followed by
roast beef with Yorkshire pudding and three vegetables,
with an apple tart from the freezer to finish the meal.

She had already told Blake that she preferred to serve
dinner single-handed while he remained at the table in

the saloon and kept an eye on everyone's glass. By dint of doing some speedy washing up between courses— the party was in good form, and would not notice a slight delay—she was able to reduce considerably the final clearing up. She had the feeling that too many after-dinner chores would hasten Blake's loss of enthusiasm for his new occupation.

Coffee and liqueurs were taken on the deck, now in moonlight. Presently Patrick asked if he might take the dinghy and row his wife ashore for a stroll before bed-time. When he asked if anyone else would like to go, his parents agreed, but Mary Harvey decided to turn in early, and her husband preferred to enjoy some more coffee and brandy.

Amalie went below to tackle the remaining washing up, hoping Blake would stay with Bob. But a few min-utes later he joined her in the galley.

'I think it's gone very smoothly. They all seem in high good humour,' he said, taking a dry tea towel from a drawer. He had quickly mastered every detail of *Sea-farer*'s stowage.

'Yes, I feel they've enjoyed their first day. Let's hope tomorrow goes equally well.'

'You've certainly fed them like princes,' he said, pat-ting his own lean, hard midriff.

'Rather dull fare for you, I'm afraid, but we can have exciting dishes when we're turning round. Blake, it's time we discussed your pay.'

'Okay.' He suggested a weekly wage a little above what her grandfather had paid his last crew.

'And what about notice?'

'Two weeks on either side. Gentleman's agreement. That's if you consider me enough of a gentleman to honour my side of the deal,' he added, with a glimmer of the mockery he had kept under hatches since his return.

'That's settled, then.' Amalie slipped her right hand out

of the loose rubber gloves she was wearing, and offered it to him.

Shaking hands reminded her of the night he had taken her out to dinner, and of what had happened after she had called him back after their first leavetaking. She felt her colour rising at the memory, and quickly turned back to the sink now empty of dishes and needing only to be rinsed and the taps wiped.

The galley restored to order, they went on deck, meeting Bob on his way to bed. 'The others are still ashore, but I'm for hitting the sack now.'

She smiled at him. 'It's a well-sprung sack, so I think you should sleep well. Goodnight, Bob.'

On deck, she sank into a chair. Blake asked what she would like to drink and she asked for a little more rosé. He had another stiff brandy.

There was a lull in the breeze, and now the voices of the others could be heard quite clearly from the beach. This was not unusual at night when sounds seemed to carry further.

They were discussing the schooner, their accommodation and the food—all in flattering terms which made reassuring hearing. Amalie and Blake listened, they could not avoid doing so, and smiled at each other. She realised with some surprise that, just for a moment, they had shared the companionableness she had had with John Lawrence.

They watched the Websters climb back into the dinghy, and Patrick take up the oars. It was then that their conversation changed to personalities, when he said, 'I wonder if our rather dishy skipper and her first mate share a cabin.'

'Of course they do, darling,' said Liza.

'Oh, no, I don't think so at all. She seems a very nice girl. Not at all *that* type,' said his mother.

Her son and daughter-in-law laughed, and her husband said dryly, 'Nice girls didn't in our day, but I rather think they do now, dear.'

'Although I must admit,' continued his daughter-in-law, 'if they are living together, they're very discreet about it. You wouldn't guess they were lovers from the way they behave. In front of us, they're quite formal.'

'As most of their customers are middle-aged people or older, probably they find it's good business not to make it too obvious,' said Patrick. 'When no one's around, she probably whips off her bra, and he puts in his ear-rings, and they have a right old rave-up.'

'He's certainly never worn ear-rings. I should have noticed the holes while we were swimming this afternoon. He couldn't be less the hippie type,' stated Mrs Webster authoritatively.

'Thank you, madam,' murmured Blake, sotto voce.

'We don't know his surname, I notice,' Mrs Webster went on. 'It wouldn't surprise me to find he's a laird or a lord. There's something distinguished about him.'

Her family broke into laughter and Blake, too, was silently laughing. Yet Amalie knew what she meant. He *did* have an air which set him apart from other men, a sort of inbuilt authority so that, in the unlikely event of *Seafarer* being shipwrecked, she knew to whom they would look to take charge of the life-raft. Not to her: to the man beside her. What a sad waste of his potential his life seemed to be, she reflected.

'Ssh, my dear! They may hear us,' said Freddie, and began to speak of something else.

'Would you like me to make it clear that we *don't* share a cabin?' asked Blake, in an amused undertone.

'They'll find that out for themselves, I expect,' Amalie said, hoping the moonlight concealed her heightened colour.

She set her alarm for sunrise, wanting to fit in a swim before the others were awake. She had always liked getting up early, being a lark rather than a night-bird.

The main hatch had been left open during the night so she made no noise going on deck. But the lifelines were open above the ladder, and she knew they had been secured. Therefore someone else was before her in the dawn-reflecting water.

It was almost certainly Blake, although she could not see him anywhere. Then, as she went down the ladder rather than diving and waking up those who were sleeping, she glimpsed his dark head on the surface, some distance away. He was floating, making no noise, watching the sunrise which was certainly something to be seen —but not his scene, she wouldn't have thought. Yet no one was all of a piece, and because a man was a rake he didn't have to be a philistine.

She wondered if he knew much poetry besides that line he had quoted close to her cheek, in a low, ardent voice which it made her shiver to remember.

Her grandfather had been a great lover of poetry, and she had searched through his books until she had found Blake's line in a poem by Andrew Marvell, *To His Coy Mistress*.

If Blake noticed her in the water, he did not come near, or even wave. Presently she saw him pulling himself up the ladder, the sun shining on his broad back which rippled with muscle as he climbed to the deck.

His trunks were stretchy Bermudas, low on the hip and long and tight on the thigh, white leaves on emerald green, and the cause of a slight double-take from Bob who wore his conventional black trunks well hitched up around his plump waist, and possibly didn't approve of men wearing anything more colourful. But on Blake's lean, lithe frame the Bermudas looked right for the West Indian setting and Bob's trunks drab and old-fashioned.

Amalie trod water, watching him rough-towel his thick curly hair and then dry off the rest of himself. Then he disappeared below.

When Amalie finished her swim, the pleasant aroma of coffee was wafting from the galley port. She had paused to squeeze out her hair when he came back on deck and, for an instant or two, his eyes took in all the smooth lines and gentle curves exposed by her brief bikini of bright blue cotton and white cord. She felt his glance like a caress on her breasts, waist and hips, and made to reach for the towel she had left on a chair.

Blake was nearer, and he forestalled her, holding it out as he might have done with an evening wrap. Having laid it lightly over her shoulders, he lifted her hair out at the back where the folds of the towel enclosed it, and the touch of his sea-cool fingers against the nape of her neck made her catch her breath.

But his tone was normal as he said, 'How about a quiet cup of coffee before the working day begins?'

'Th-that would be very nice, thank you.'

Was it she alone who had felt a stirring of the senses? Or had he felt it, too, but would not now follow it up because, to quote Marvell again, he made it a rule to *gather the flowers, but spare the buds.*

Waiting for him to come back with her mug of coffee, Amalie found herself wishing that she were five years older and infinitely more sophisticated; in fact a flower to be plucked by the strong brown fingers which had brushed her neck a moment ago. But at not-quite-twenty, she knew that it was too soon to give up her secret dreams of finding a man who combined Blake's powerful attraction with Roderick's niceness.

When he brought her the coffee she noticed that he had shaved and changed into white cotton shorts.

'There are sounds of life stirring,' he told her. 'They may like a dip before breakfast. Shall we have it on deck?' When she nodded, he said, 'I'll lay the table.'

For breakfast she gave them chilled orange juice, and bacon and eggs with mushrooms on fried bread, followed by toast or hot rolls with black cherry jam or marmalade.

It was after lunch, by which time they had arrived at the second night's anchorage, a good spot for snorkeling, that while the others were relaxing, Blake asked her if she would mind if he used the radiotelephone.

'I'll pay for my calls, naturally. There are a couple of people with whom I like to keep in touch.'

'That's all right. Any time,' she agreed.

The R/T equipment on *Seafarer* had been installed in her grandfather's quarters, always open during the day. It was fitted with a device which emitted a special alarm tone if someone within its range was sending out a distress signal. By calling the nearest marine operator, it was possible to be linked with the international telephone system and make long-distance calls. This had been a useful facility for some of her grandfather's charterers if they happened to be wealthy men who liked to be constantly in touch with their businesses or stockbrokers.

Blake made his calls while everyone else was bathing, except Joan Webster who was dozing under the awning.

For dinner they set up the barbecue on the beach. Some boats had barbecues aboard, but John Lawrence had thought them potentially dangerous, and almost certainly damaging to his well-kept teak decks.

After the barbecue they were joined by six other people from a charter boat sharing the anchorage. Next day, Amalie's party took a rather touching delight in the fact that, bound for the same destination as the second vessel, *Seafarer* soon overhauled her in spite of being last to weigh anchor.

Many rolls of film were expended in shots of them all at the wheel or in other nautical poses. Bob had a ciné camera with which he filmed all their activities from exploring a small island's market, to drinking pre-luncheon aperitifs while up to their waists in the warm sea.

It had been Angela Scott's suggestion that the penultimate night of the cruise should be spent near a famous hotel with a restaurant and night-club open to non-residents.

'Unless they don't fancy the idea, it will give you an evening off and then a chance to dress up. The place has a very good Pan band, and the floor show includes limbo dancing which most tourists like to see once,' she had advised Amalie.

The Websters and Harveys received the suggestion with enthusiasm. Amalie had thought they might like to be on their own for a change, but they insisted that she and Blake must also go, and be their guests.

'I'll be frank and admit that, when we first met you, I had certain reservations about entrusting our safety to a captain who was of the fair sex, and as young as you, Amalie,' said Bob. 'But you've given us a splendid holiday which we hope to repeat another year, and I think we all realise now you're a very competent skipper.'

She beamed at him. 'Thank you, Bob. And you've all been marvellous passengers.'

'It certainly seems a great life compared to mine, stuck in an office most of the year,' said Patrick wistfully. 'You have to be licensed, I suppose?'

It was Blake who answered him. 'Not everywhere. But it's sense to have a yachtmaster's ticket, and I got mine without any trouble. I'm sure you could, too, if you wanted to. It's largely a matter of mastering simple navigation.'

'Oh, don't encourage him, Blake,' Liza exclaimed, in mock horror. 'Maybe when we retire, but not for many years yet. I don't fancy bringing up children on a boat. One would be forever on pins in case they'd fallen overboard. It's a wonderful life for a holiday—but not for everyday. For you two, perhaps, but not for Patrick and me.'

Did she mean to imply that they were also a pair? Amalie wondered. Or had they all realised by now that she and Blake did not sleep together? Perhaps not. He kept his cabin so immaculate that it still looked unoccupied, and usually during the day all the doors were hooked open, and the privacy curtains drawn back, to increase the circulation of air, also helped by the stainless steel wind chutes pushed out of the ports whenever they were at anchor.

'Have you really got your ticket?' she asked Blake, later in the day.

'I told you, I don't often lie,' he replied, smiling slightly. 'It seemed a useful qualification, and not too difficult to come by. I can fly a plane, too. You'd be surprised at my talents.'

'Less now than when we first met. But why not make more of your life, instead of just swanning around as that old man's bodyguard and now crewing for me? I feel you're wasting yourself.'

'Maybe, but living like this I shan't get an ulcer or an early coronary, shall I?'

'No, that's true, I suppose,' she agreed. 'I feel a bit sorry for Patrick, saddled by a mortgage and so on, and not free to do as he likes until he retires.'

'It's Liza who's put the saddle on him. It's her ambitions, not his own, which will drive him on,' he said cynically. 'Not very far, I shouldn't think. He's not a potential top man.'

'How on earth can you say that?' she asked, a little indignant that he should presume to pass judgment.

'You forget I've lived with top men. Cheiro Androcles had a mind like a razor. If you'd known him, you'd have recognised the difference between him and these three men, even though they're not doing too badly if they can afford to charter cruise.'

'Perhaps I ought not to say so, as I'm under an obligation to her, but it seems to me that his last wife was not as well chosen as these men's wives are for them.'

'Ah, yes—Stella,' Blake murmured ruminatively. 'I

think you're too young, and the wrong sex, to understand why he married her.'

'Do you understand it?'

They were in the galley together where Amalie was cutting melted chocolate into squares for a special gâteau she had planned for the last night dinner. Blake had been slicing a lemon to put in a bag in the deck box, on hand for the gin and tonics which Patrick and Liza liked to drink about six.

Now, leaning against a worktop, out of Amalie's way but watching her deft strokes, he said, 'Most people's follies are understandable and forgivable if one knows what lies behind them. In his last year, Cheiro liked to talk about his past. He had married young, choosing an ugly girl ten years older than himself for the sake of her substantial dowry. It became the basis of his fortune, and she also gave him three sons. She was never desirable to him, but he said he was never unfaithful, as most men would have been in his shoes. However, after her death he began to regret his self-denial, and to want the young wife he had missed. So he married Stella who was all Cosima had not been. Soon afterwards he became ill. He never had much pleasure from her, except to buy for her the jewels which would have been wasted on Cosima. It was an old man's whim with which Stella was happy to co-operate,' he added sardonically.

'How sad! What a waste of a life. I wonder if Cosima loved him?' Amalie murmured.

'I should doubt it. Greek girls of her generation weren't brought up on romantic daydreams. She lived in great comfort, proud of her sons and interested in all their off-spring.'

'What about the old man's favourite? The one who has inherited Paradise and most of the money? What kind of man is he?'

'Not a bad sort. Why? Would you like to meet him?

I daresay it could be arranged. He comes out here now and again.'

'Does he? Well, I don't think I'll trouble you to arrange an introduction,' she said, smiling. 'I'm not in the market for rich men. I *was* bred on romantic daydreams, and for the time being I'm sticking to them. Mr Blunt said Androcles was known to be a great ladies' man. A married one, or a bachelor?'

'He's unmarried. For him, being born into money, it isn't necessary to marry well. His difficulty would be to find a woman who wants him and not his possessions.'

'Is he unattractive?' asked Amalie.

'Not being a female I wouldn't know,' said Blake, shrugging. 'But most of the girls he encounters would make out they liked him even if they couldn't stand him.'

'Yes, I suppose that can be a hazard, if one is exceptionally rich. At least when you bowl them over you know it's your charm which does it.'

Besides the black and white dress she had worn for her date with Blake, Amalie had a more glamorous one which she put on to go to the hotel. It was made of misty green cotton, the low bodice bound with silk to match the silk shoestring straps. It had a full swirling skirt, and a triangular wrap to cover her shoulders if the night should grow cool.

She arrived on deck in the wake of the three other women, but with her shoes in her hand as she knew from experience that climbing a boarding ladder in high heels was, if not impossible, hazardous.

Blake went down the ladder first, and helped the four women descend. Amalie felt his hands grasp her waist, ready to hold her if she should miss her footing, as Mrs Webster had nearly done.

With the outboard fitted, it did not take long to motor gently towards the jetty at the bottom of the hotel garden. The palms were strung with coloured lanterns; the sound of a steel band could be heard in the distance. Amalie felt pleased and excited; pleased because the cruise had been successful, and excited because, before the evening was over, she would have had Blake's arm around her, if only on the dance floor.

She knew she ought not to be looking forward to this, but she couldn't help it—even if it were playing with fire. The antagonism she had felt towards him after being kissed, and again when he had reappeared, had largely subsided during the week. There were things about him she couldn't approve of, but he had been an excellent crew, doing all that was required of him and more—only that morning she had found him in the bosun's locker, checking the spare shackles—and, as yet, he did not appear bored.

She did not sit next to him at dinner. He was between Joan and Mary, and she between Freddie and Bob. The table was a round one, lit by several candles with glass shades to stop them flickering, with a centrepiece of tropical blossoms floating in a shallow container.

The menu being *à la carte*, Amalie was able to indulge her liking for more exotic dishes than she had served to her guests. She and Blake chose the Creole curry, the young couple lobster Newburg, and their elders settled for steaks.

Blake seemed to know a good deal about the steel band which was playing for them. He pointed out the different types of pan; at the side of the big oil drums called tune-booms with a range of three or four notes, and the somewhat shorter cello-pans with as many as six notes. Between these came the guitar-pans with fourteen notes each, and then, in the centre, the ping-pongs tuned to play more than twice as many.

'When did it start, this kind of music?' Mary asked him.

'It grew out of the mixture of cultures in Trinidad and Tobago. The drumming came first from Africa with the slaves from the Yoruba and Mandingo nations. Their god was Shango, the Lord of Thunder and Lightning, whom they worshipped with special sacred drums. As slaves they weren't allowed to practise their religion, and the only drumming was at Cannes Brulée when the sugar canes were burned. They used to have a torchlight procession, with drummers, which gradually developed into the present-day Carnival.'

'That's something we ought to see some time,' put in Bob. 'What time of year does it take place?'—looking at Amalie.

Never having been to Trinidad, she didn't know. But Blake did.

He said, 'It lasts for two days before Lent, but the preparations take months.' Resuming his answer to Mary's question, he went on, 'After the slaves came the workers from India with their goatskin Taza drums, and that was followed by an entirely Trinidadian development, the Tamboo-bamboo band. The origin of Pan as such goes back to the 1930s, but who struck the first note is arguable. One story is that a bamboo-player called Mussel Rat broke his bamboo and kept up the rhythm by beating the empty tank of an old motor car in the back yard where he was playing.'

'Blake is so widely travelled and well informed, I'm surprised he isn't a skipper with his own boat,' said Mary to Amalie, later.

The meal was over and they were alone at the table while Blake was dancing with Liza and Patrick with his mother.

It was not the first time she and Joan had tried to pump Amalie for information about him, and her evasive replies—because most of what little she knew might not enhance their opinion of him—only served to fan their curiosity. Their opinion of her, she suspected, was tinged with a certain dubiety as to whether they could approve of a girl of nineteen and a man about ten years her senior living together, in either sense of the term.

Having danced with the three other women, Blake
took Amalie on to the floor for a lively number which involved no close physical contact.

In spite of her lack of ear by musicians' standards,
there was nothing wrong with her sense of rhythm, and
Blake was a better partner than Freddie and Bob, who,
perhaps to compensate for an inward selfconsciousness,
were inclined to overdo their performance of the current
dances.

The end of the dance found them on the far side of the
floor from their party's table and, as the floor remained
crowded, they were still moving round the edge when
the next number started. This time it was slower and
sweeter, with a girl singer purring a lyric which began
'Come closer to me ...'

Amalie hoped Blake might catch her by the wrist and
draw her back among the dancers. But he didn't, and she
lacked the courage to turn and say, 'Shall we dance this?'

The song was the last before the floor-show began
with a dimming of lights and the rattle of unseen
maracas.

While everyone else's attention was focussed on the
limbo dancers as they writhed and wriggled under a bar
which was placed at lower and lower levels by their
gaudily-costumed attendants, she found her own eyes
drawn to Blake who was sitting, half turned from the
table, between her and the colourful spectacle. He was
not blocking her view, but his position made it easy for
her to study him without anyone noticing that it was his
hawk-like profile, and not the show, which held her
gaze.

Suddenly, as if he could feel someone staring at him,
he turned his head. Their eyes met across the table, the
candlelight making his blue ones arrestingly brilliant in
the dark brown, inscrutable mask of his un-English face.

She gave him an uncertain smile which he did not return before he turned back to the show and joined in the applause for the final most difficult feat which he had just missed.

Afterwards, when the band had returned, Amalie was surprised to be asked to dance by a young man from the next table. He was an American of about her own age, holidaying with his sisters, their parents, and one set of grandparents. He had taken her for the daughter of either the Websters or the Harveys.

Although she found Steve very pleasant, with the easy, outgoing manners of so many of his countrymen, Amalie did not want to spend the rest of the evening dancing with him, although this seemed his intention. Except by a pointed brush-off, which she could not bring herself to give him, there seemed no way to avoid going on being his partner.

Eventually she came off the floor to find the four older people on the point of going back to the schooner.

'But Liza and Patrick are staying, and there's no need for you to come with us. You go on enjoying yourself, dear. At your age one can afford to burn the candle at both ends,' said Mary.

'Oh, but I——' she began.

Blake said, 'I'll be back at the jetty to pick you up in an hour—or later, if you'd prefer it'—speaking to Patrick.

'No, an hour would be fine. We don't want to turn in too late or we may miss our pre-breakfast swim, and we've only two more to go,' was Patrick's reply.

So Amalie found that, unless she made an issue of the matter, she was forced to stay at the dance.

She wondered if, but for Steve's intervention, Blake would have danced with her again. Perhaps, having ferried the others back to *Seafarer*, he felt it his duty to stay with them. Or could it be that he preferred their company to hers?

It seemed a long hour before, having said goodnight to Steve and his family, the three of them strolled back to the jetty. They found Blake lounging on a seat under a palm-thatched roof which by day made a shady place from which to admire the view or wait for a boat.

Although it was now after one, the steel band would play for an hour yet, and lights and the sound of voices came from most of the yachts lying at anchor off the beach.

'Next week this will seem like a dream,' remarked Patrick, his arm round his wife and his eyes on the motionless schooner, as they skimmed across the still water. 'What about a swim now, by moonlight?'

'Yes, why not?' Liza agreed. 'What about you two?'

'Why not?' Blake echoed. 'Amalie?'

She had always liked swimming at night, and she wanted to speak to him. She nodded. 'A good idea.'

'As long as we keep it quiet,' was Blake's qualification. 'The others have turned in.'

He and Patrick were already in the sea when the girls reappeared, having agreed it would be a good idea to take off their eye make-up beforehand.

At night the water felt warmer than it did by day, and the ripples made by their strokes made a shifting pattern of moon-gleams on the white hull. Presently the young Websters decided to swim as far as the beach and back, and Blake said there would be a nightcap ready when they returned.

When he climbed aboard, Amalie followed.

'You might have rescued me from that young man,' she said, in a low voice, as they dried themselves.

'I thought you were enjoying his company. It seemed to be something to encourage.'

'Encourage? Why? I shan't be seeing him again.'

'No, but it made clear to the others that ours is only a working connection. Had I rescued you, as you put it, they might have thought I was being possessive. I'd rather not be taken for a cradle-snatcher.'

'I'm not seventeen, Blake, and you're not much older than Patrick.'

'No, but it's obvious they're curious about our relationship, particularly the two women. These are very respectable people who are more on the side of Mrs Whitehouse and the censorship lobby than of the permissive brigade. Bob is going to show the film he's taken to all their friends, some of whom may become future customers. It's better for them to regard you as the kind of nice, wholesome girl they would wish their daughters to be, than one of the kind whose behaviour they have to accept outwardly, but don't really like in their hearts.'

'One would almost think you were one of them—the respectable brigade.'

'No, but I know how their minds work. Although commercially they aren't an important market now, they are the main body of your market. They want to be sure of their safety; they want to eat familiar food; and they don't want to be embarrassed by the kind of avant-garde couple Patrick described that first night.'

'I agree, but it's going a bit far to leave me stuck with that boy in order to prove your indifference,' she protested.

'That boy looked twenty to me.'

'He may be, I didn't ask him. He was nice, but just not my type.'

'It takes time to find that out. Your type will turn up some day. I'd better get those nightcaps organised.'

He left her on deck, annoyed by his fraternal manner. Amalie hadn't liked it before, when he'd wanted to rush her into bed, but neither did she like this change to an elder-brotherly attitude. What she wanted was something between: neither hot lust nor cool indifference. But perhaps with a man like Blake there could be no middle ground. She remembered the strange, fierce look he had turned on her during the floor-show, and she knew she couldn't begin to understand him.

Thirty-six hours later, she said goodbye to the first party, and turned her mind to the many jobs to be tackled before the arrival of the next party.

By the time she returned from the airport Blake had thoroughly scrubbed out the dinghy and begun to wash down the hull. He said he would like to take a couple of hours off to see if there might be mail waiting for him at Paradise. He would then return to finish the hull and clean the decks, while Amalie turned out the cabins.

'And, under your reforming influence, I'll return that bottle of bubbly,' he added, with a grin.

Shortly after his departure she heard a tattoo on the hull and put her head out of the hatch to find Roderick coming aboard.

'Hello there. How did it go? We're only just back. Mother asks if you'd like to have coffee before we start on the turn-round.'

'Hello, Roderick. It went like a dream. Yes, I'd love to come over and see her. How was your cruise—successful?' she asked.

'I think the charterers enjoyed it. We found them a bit heavy going. Our next lot will be more congenial: an American surgeon and his family, all enthusiastic small-boat sailors who love sailing *Carrageen* for us. We relax half the time they're aboard. This will be their third cruise with us.'

'Oh, really? That's interesting. My next lot are medical people; he's a consultant in London, and she's an ex-theatre Sister. I looked them up in Grandpa's notes. They've been on one previous cruise, but it was about five years ago. Now, as well as their teenage twins, they're bringing a baby and a French au pair girl.'

'That's great,' said Roderick. 'Because I thought this

time we might cruise together, and if our passengers
mesh, so much the better.'

'I don't think two medical men would necessarily want
to talk shop on holiday, would they? I imagine they like
to forget their profession for a while.'

'Yes, I daresay they do, but they'll be on the same
general wavelength, and the Reinhardts have three teenage children to chum up with your couple's twins.'

By this time they had come alongside *Carrageen*
where Lady Scott was waiting to greet Amalie with a
smiling, 'Hello, my dear. How did it go? You've been
very much on our minds, hasn't she, Roderick?'

'Yes, we've been on hot bricks,' he agreed. 'What's this
crew like, the Greek woman sent you?'

'Oh, he couldn't have been more efficient. He has a
yachtmaster's ticket, and he's very good on the social
side. But he isn't the man they were sending. That plan
went awry, so Blake has been standing in for him. You
remember I told you about him—the one who was Androcles' bodyguard.'

'That man! But I thought you disliked him? He was a
fast worker, you said,' was Roderick's mother's reaction
to this piece of news.

'He seemed to be at the beginning, but he hasn't been
since. He's been invaluable.'

'He can't have had much opportunity while the charter
party were with you. What about during the turn-round?
Is he sleeping on board with you tonight?'

'As far as I know he is, yes. As he did the first night
he arrived. But there's a good lock on my door, and he's
not the type to break in.'

'Possibly not, but it's an undesirable situation, even
in this day and age. A man you don't know from Adam,
who may be all right when he's sober, but who might
become extremely objectionable if he'd had too much to
drink. I think you should sleep with us, Amalie, during
the turn-round.'

'Yes, so do I,' her son seconded. 'A chap who's already made one pass will sooner or later make another.'

'No, he won't—not now,' she assured them. 'He didn't realise at the time that I was ... well, rather old-fashioned. Why not come to supper and meet him? We're having a shrimp jambalaya. There's plenty for four.'

'We'd be delighted,' said Angela. 'If you're providing the main course, let me bring the pudding.'

'And if we don't take to your crew, we'll bring you back here for the night,' Roderick added firmly.

CHAPTER FOUR

It was not usual, Amalie discovered during supper that evening, for the charterers to be met at the airport. Usually the onus of finding a taxi to bring them to the harbour was on them. It was only when they stepped aboard that their welfare became her responsibility.

Nor had she known, until Roderick told her—and it wasn't a hazard which applied to her—that if a charter yacht took a passenger from one country to another, and he turned out to lack either funds or papers, it would be the skipper's duty to keep him aboard or return him to the port of embarkation.

'But that's a risk which is more likely to crop up when a charter boat moves, say, from the Mediterranean to here, or from here to the Pacific,' he explained.

Amalie listened attentively to all he could tell her about the business. For the first part of the meal the talk had been general among the four of them. But presently two separate conversations evolved; one devoted to matter nautical between Roderick and herself, and another between his mother and Blake. They, from one or two snatches which impinged on her, seemed to be discussing London museums and art galleries.

After supper, while she and Roderick were washing up, and the others had gone to sit on deck, she asked what he thought of Blake.

'Too smooth for my liking,' was his answer.

'Smooth?' she echoed, her forehead wrinkling in puzzlement. 'What makes you say that?' It had not struck her that Blake's good manners were over-urbane.

'It didn't take him long to pick up Mother's wavelength, did it? And to draw her out on all her pet subjects. That's typical of a smooth operator. You'll see: she'll have found him charming.'

'Perhaps they have interests in common. They seemed to be talking about paintings. Was your mother an artist at one time?'

'No, she collected certain types of paintings. Most were sold when they moved out here, but she still has a collection of portrait miniatures kept in the bank as insurance against a rainy day.' He paused before going on, 'My parents' marriage was rather a strange one in some ways. They were very happy together, in spite of being absolute opposites. I suppose it worked because Mother subjugated her interest to my father's. To look at her now, living here, you'd never guess, would you, that her natural milieu is Knightsbridge and Bond Street?'

'No, I took her to be a born country person, or at least an outdoor one.'

'Oh, that's all superimposed. She enjoys the sun and the sea, and I don't think she's actively unhappy. But, at root, she's a collector and connoisseur. She adores going round all the galleries, and poking about in antique shops. Eventually, I expect, she'll go back and live in some little mews house in Chelsea, and pick up with all her old cronies. Meanwhile, poor love, she's lumbered with housekeeping for me and the charterers.'

Before they left the galley to join the others, Amalie said, 'But even if you think Blake smooth, you do see it isn't necessary for me to take refuge from him during turn-rounds?'

'He doesn't seem that sort of ape,' Roderick conceded. 'But I still don't like the idea of your being here alone with him.'

'All the same, Roderick, please don't suggest I should sleep on board *Carrageen*. It would make for an awkward atmosphere if I seemed to distrust him to that extent. He can be very sardonic when he chooses.'

'He's got no damned right to be sardonic! He's a hired

hand. He shouldn't forget it.'

'An unusual hired hand,' she told him. 'He was educated at Winchester.'

'Did he tell you that? That convinces me he's a con man,' said Roderick. 'One doesn't announce things of that sort. The fact might emerge, indirectly, but no one would actually say he was at Eton or whatever.'

'He didn't announce it. It did emerge indirectly. You really don't like him, do you?'

'No, I feel in my bones he's a crook—or at least not a straight type.'

As they came on deck, Blake broke off what he was saying and rose from his chair until Amalie was seated. Before discussing him with Roderick she would have seen this as normal mannerliness, but Roderick seemed to have infected her with his own suspicion, and she found herself wondering if, in so informal a setting, such courtesies could be overdone.

Perhaps it took a man to judge a man. Roderick, known to her grandfather before her, and whose background held no mysteries, was someone she liked and could trust. If his instinct told him that Blake was a shady character, ought she not to share his mistrust?

The Scotts left about eleven, having a long list of chores to be done the next day.

'A nice woman, that,' Blake remarked, as their visitors' dinghy disappeared from view round the bows of one of the vessels between *Seafarer*'s berth and their own.

'And Roderick?' Amalie asked, being curious to know if the antagonism had been mutual.

'Takes after his father, I'd say. A man of action, not an intellectual like his mother. But a sound and sensible sort of chap—much smitten by the newcomer to their circle,' he added, with an amused glance.

'By me? Oh, nonsense! He's only being friendly.'

'His type don't rush their fences, like some of us. You'd suit each other pretty well, and then Lady Scott could go back to where she belongs.'

'Did she tell you she didn't belong here?'

'Not in so many words. Her enthusiasms make it obvious this isn't really her scene. But she was a devoted wife, and now an affectionate mother, so I suppose she finds it rewarding to stay on until her son marries.'

'I should never have suspected you of such a match-making turn of mind, Blake,' said Amalie lightly.

'It's the thought I read in *her* mind while you were dishing up that excellent jambalaya, and demonstrating that you could provide her son with all the creature comforts to which he's accustomed.'

'A man needs more than a good cook to make him happy.'

'Not much more. An enthusiastic partner in bed, good temper rather than bad—that's all it would take to make Roderick happy.'

'And you? Would that satisfy you?'

'If I were the marrying kind, I daresay it would.'

'You don't have to emphasise that you aren't for my benefit. I'm the last person to harbour romantic illusions about you. You dashed them the first time we met, and even more so the second time.'

'Never mind, I'm sure Roderick won't. He'll do it all just as you'd like it. Go to bed and have sweet dreams about him,' he said in an oddly harsh tone. 'I'm going ashore for an hour.'

She was still awake when he came back. But, if he had been in a bar, he had not drunk enough to be clumsy coming aboard. Asleep, Amalie would not have been wakened, unless by the tap in the washroom which could be heard faintly from her cabin.

The harbour at night was never altogether silent, nor was any ship wholly noiseless. But soon, between decks on the schooner, all was as quiet as it could be.

Amalie, still wide awake, lay wondering if Roderick was right in his judgment of Blake, and Blake in his judgment of Roderick. The younger man's suggestion that they should do a joint cruise lent some colour to Blake's surmise. She wondered if it was a good plan, and if the Reinhardts and the Kingsleys would jell as Roderick had forecast. Wondering if meals for the baby were going to present any problems, finally she fell asleep.

By the time the Kingsleys arrived, *Seafarer* had been springcleaned from stem to stern, refuelled, her supplies replenished, her berths made up with clean linen, and her deck-ice replaced.

At Amalie's request Blake brought the family aboard, having first introduced himself to them, and explained the death of John Lawrence.

These preliminaries took place on the quay, and gave her a chance to study the family before she met them. Philip Kingsley looked about fifty, tall, thin, with grey but thick hair. His wife, perhaps ten years his junior, was also thin and long-legged, as were the two lanky twin boys. Only the baby, at present dangling over its father's forearm and reaching with pink starfish hands for the tag on its mother's shoulder-bag, was a plump, downy-haired little thing of uncertain sex.

They had all been piled in one taxi, the father in front with the baby, and the mother behind with her two sons squeezed between her and the other member of their ménage. This was a dark-eyed ash-blonde, somewhat older than Amalie had expected their au pair to be. She looked at least twenty-five, and her tight white skirt and four-inch heels suggested she might have some difficulty in coming aboard.

'Good morning. Welcome aboard. Shall I take the baby?' said Amalie, smiling down at them as the dinghy came alongside.

Mr Kingsley passed up the infant, who showed no sign of alarm at being handed to a stranger, and promptly attempted to seize the chain round Amalie's neck.

'Oh, careful—don't let her break it,' warned Mrs Kingsley, seeing this.

'It's only a gilt one.' Amalie gently deflected the exploring fingers. 'What's her name?'

'Josephine. How do you do, Miss Heron?' Mr Kingsley stepped on to the deck, and shook hands with her.

'How nice to be back on board *Seafarer*, but we're all very sad to hear about your grandfather,' said his wife as she also shook hands. 'Tim and Chris were only ten when we did our first cruise with him, but he let them take turns at the wheel and they've never forgotten it.'

'I hope you'll enjoy this cruise, too,' said Amalie, smiling at the boys. 'How shall I know which of you is Chris and which Tim?'—for they were identical twins and, although not dressed alike now, would be difficult to distinguish in the water.

'You can tell when you get to know us,' said one boy. 'And at the moment I've got a cut finger'—displaying the plaster on it. 'I'm Chris.'

While she was greeting the boys, Amalie was aware of laughter rising from the dinghy, and of Blake saying something in French.

Mr Kingsley having retrieved his daughter from her, she glanced over the side to see how the French girl was going to cope with the boarding ladder.

Presumably on Blake's advice, she had already taken off her sandals, and now was hitching up her skirt and displaying a pair of rounded thighs, already sun-tanned.

With one foot on the ladder, she paused, saying something which clearly meant, 'Oh, my skirt won't stay up by itself, and I need my hands for the ladder. What shall I do?'

His reply must have been, 'I'll hold it for you.' Rehitching her skirt for her, he held it, and her hips, while she mounted the rungs. As she reached the deck, his height enabled him to give her a pat on the bottom before letting go.

The girl looked down. '*Merci, Capitaine.*'

Her eyes held laughter, as did his.

'This is Hélène Marchand, who is staying with us for a year and helping me to look after Josephine,' said Mrs Kingsley.

The two girls shook hands, and Hélène said 'Hello' in response to Amalie's greeting in French.

It was not her only word of English. It was soon clear she spoke it well.

As with the first charter party, they had lunch before leaving harbour. *Carrageen* had already left, but they saw her again some hours later when they reached their first anchorage. Her passengers, the Americans, were already disporting in the water, and as soon as they could the Kingsleys followed their example, leaving Amalie to dandle Josephine.

Very soon the two lots of passengers were exchanging comments on the warmth and clarity of the sea and getting to know each other. Neither Roderick nor his mother was in sight. Probably Angela Scott was starting supper preparations and perhaps he was helping her.

The first of *Seafarer*'s bathers to return on board was Blake who said, as he swung into view, 'I'll take over the baby. You have a dip now.'

He rubbed himself down and reached out both hands for the infant. When Amalie hesitated, he said, 'She'll be safe. My sister has had four of these, and I've never dropped one yet.'

Josephine went into his charge as blithely as, so far, she had accepted all the day's new experiences. Now naked but for a Liberty print cotton sun-hat, she sat perched on Blake's strong dark forearm and reached up a hand to grab at his thick curly hair. He laughed and eluded her grasp, and spoke to her gently in what presumably was Greek. For a moment there was on his face an expression which Amalie, watching, found curiously moving. Clearly he was capable of tenderness, but perhaps only with girls of Josephine's age, never with grown ones. Even as she watched, he turned his head and the expression changed to the more familiar look of predatory appraisal as Hélène, her white bikini now wet and transparent, came back on board.

Later, passing the Kingsleys' cabin while it was closed off only by the privacy curtain, Amalie heard Harriet Kingsley remark, 'At least Hélène won't be bored now.'

'Got her eye on the big fellow, has she? She may be poaching on the granddaughter's territory. What's the set-up? Any idea?'

'She left them together, I noticed, when we were swimming. I think he just helps run the boat. Not that it would bother Hélène——'

Here, Amalie passed out of earshot.

She did not see Roderick until, after dinner, he came across in his tender to invite the party on *Seafarer* to have drinks aboard *Carrageen*.

'I must stay in case Josephine cries. Will you keep me company, Blake?' Hélène asked him, after the Kingsleys had accepted the invitation.

'With pleasure,' he answered.

'Where is Brigitte Bardot?' asked Roderick when, later, he had an opportunity to draw Amalie aside.

'She's minding the baby.'

'And Blake is minding her, I gather?'

She nodded.

He said, 'Mrs Kingsley must be very sure of her husband to have a siren of that order around the house. I only saw a blonde head in the water, but earlier Mrs Reinhardt was teasing her husband about the terrific *oeillade* the French girl had given him. Shall I get one, too?'

'Probably. Her name is Hélène. She's not an ordinary au pair, she's Mr Kingsley's niece. His sister married a Frenchman.'

'Oh, well, she'll deflect any amorous impulses which Blake might have vented on you,' said Roderick cheerfully. 'Have you met our spry septuagenarian?'

He introduced her to the senior of the two Mrs Reinhardts who, slim and chic in a scarlet shirt and white pants, was, unbelievably, nearer to eighty than seventy.

The Reinhardt's daughters were aged from twelve to sixteen, three long-haired sea sprites as much at home in the water as the Kingsley twins with whom they had already passed beyond any initial shyness and were talking about snorkeling.

By the time *Seafarer*'s passengers returned to their own vessel, it was clear that the adults of both families were as much en rapport as Roderick had hoped, and the youngsters were keen to meet again.

Blake and Hélène were not together when the others returned. It seemed likely they had been until shortly beforehand, but probably Blake had seen the dinghy returning. He was in the galley, making cocoa for the twins. Hélène was elsewhere.

'We've fixed up a race with *Carrageen*,' Amalie heard Philip tell him. 'It seems they're heading the same way as we are tomorrow. Would you back us to beat them?'

She did not hear Blake's reply because, just then, Harriet spoke to her.

Later, when she thought everyone else had turned in, Blake joined her where she had been leaning over the bow rails, following the catenary of the anchor chain until it was lost in the shadowy depths of five fathoms.

'Is this meeting a happy accident? Or could it be that Scott was lying in wait for you?' he asked, in a teasing undertone.

'Perhaps I was following him,' she answered lightly, straightening her spine.

'I doubt it. You're much too demure to make the running with any man.'

Demure! It made her sound a shy, timid mouse like Miss Phoebe in *Quality Street*, a play they had acted at school.

'Unlike Hélène.' The retort was out before she could check it.

'Claws, Amalie?' he said softly. 'Hélène has nothing that you haven't got. She advertises it more. Are we going to win this race tomorrow? I shouldn't advise it. Scott isn't the type to care for being beaten by a woman.'

'Are you?' she enquired, looking up at him.

'Mine isn't that kind of ego. I'm taller and stronger than you are. I don't have to be your superior in all the ways there are.'

'I shouldn't think Roderick does either.' Yet she knew he was right: Roderick wouldn't like to be beaten.

'Why don't you and the twins do the sailing? Then I shan't be involved,' she suggested.

'Okay, we'll do that. Goodnight.'

He touched her cheek with his forefinger, and turned away and went below.

It was the kind of affectionate gesture he might make to one of the Reinhardt girls, when he got to know them. Amalie remembered his brown hand patting the apple-like curve of Hélène's small, round behind. But she did not want that from him either. What did she want from him?

Nothing.

Nothing, she told herself.

For a time, the next morning, it seemed that he and the boys might win the race. But on the last lap they lost it.

When the Scotts and the Reinhardts came aboard *Seafarer*, for a combined buffet lunch and to be congratulated on their victory, only Amalie knew that Blake had lost it deliberately.

Aided by Archer Reinhardt, an experienced yachtsman, Roderick ought to have had no trouble in beating Blake with his two willing but inexperienced young deck hands. But in fact Blake's handling of the schooner had been masterly, making Amalie wonder if he had some experience of ocean racing. Only at the end, and unbeknown to the twins' parents who were devotees of water sports but not sailing people, he had given the race away.

Puzzled by his motive, later, when they were alone, she asked, 'Why did you give the race away?'

'I think the result was the right one. We should have had a handicap.'

'Why?'

'*Seafarer* is the better boat. You didn't mind losing, did you?'

'No, I didn't mind that. It was such a super morning. I haven't enjoyed myself so much since I was here before with Grandpa. Who was it whose idea of heaven was "eating *pâté de foie gras* to the sound of trumpets"? I think mine would be to sail on and on, for ever, with a breeze and a sea like we had today. No trumpets: just the sound of the wind in the sails, and the sun on one's face, and the spray flying up from the bow wave like millions of diamonds.'

As she stopped, she felt slightly embarrassed by the fervour in her own voice. But for once Blake's eyes were not amused. He said, 'You've really found your niche, haven't you? You would hat to have to give it up?'

'I couldn't bear to—not now. Sometimes in England I used to wonder if I'd exaggerated it in my mind ... remembering it as better than it was. But I hadn't. The reality is better than my memory. I want to spend the rest of my life here. Living on a boat and making a living by chartering means as much to me as playing the cello does to Tabby.'

'Providing you don't lose your heart to a landsman, I

shouldn't think you ever will have to give it up.'

'I hope not. To live in a house after this would feel like being caged.'

'Even a house such as Paradise?'

'I'm never likely to live in a house of that order,' said Amalie dryly. 'And yes, even in a mansion, I'm sure I shouldn't be as happy as I am on *Seafarer*. This is definitely my place in the world.'

'And Scott's as well.'

'Are you still on that tack?' she said lightly.

'It's plain sailing for you at present, but it isn't always for anyone. I think you need someone to look after you, and Scott seems a suitable candidate.'

'If we happened to fall in love with each other.'

'Oh, love ...' Blake's tone was dismissive. 'You have a great deal in common, and almost any healthy young male and female can please each other in bed. Marriage lasts too long to be based on some crazy idea that only one man in the world, or one woman, can be the right one.'

'I don't believe that. But I do think love is much more than a matter of mutual interests. Lady Scott and her husband were happy without common interests.'

'In my observation, happiness is a matter of accepting life as it is rather than as it might be,' he answered. 'I've noticed that most of the people who marry and stay married are those who know they aren't perfect, and don't expect perfection in their partner.'

'I'm surprised that you've given so much thought to it,' she commented. 'I should have imagined that marriage was the very last thing to interest you.'

'It's the way most people still live. My way, too, perhaps—one of these days.'

'But not while girls like Hélène are around, and available.'

As she had the night before, Amalie at once regretted this remark. It was not like her to be catty, but all after-

noon the French girl had been posing and posturing for
Blake's benefit; and, for a reason she could not explain
to herself Amalie had found it irritating.

Her rejoinder made Blake laugh. 'I wonder why girls
who aren't generous with their favours invariably seem
to resent the ones who are? You should be grateful to
Hélène. If she weren't around, I might have my eye on
you—and you wouldn't like that, would you, Amalie?'
He grinned, and walked off.

The next day Roderick kissed her.

Everyone on the two boats, with the exception of old
Mrs Reinhardt and Josephine, had been on a snorkeling
expedition along a particularly beautiful section of reef.

Hélène had not snorkeled before, and had needed a
great deal of help with the adjustment of her mask, and
to overcome her alleged nervousness. All the children
did their best to reassure her, demonstrating how easy
it was, and how even a complete non-swimmer couldn't
drown with a mask on. But only by holding Blake's hand
was she able to overcome her timidity.

With the twins and the girls forming one shoal, and
the two sets of parents another, it was natural that
Amalie and Roderick should find themselves swimming
together, and drawing each other's attention to a black
and bright orange Rock Beauty, or a glowingly blue
Queen Angelfish, as they swam over the strange coral
gardens under the sea.

When at last they were sated with gazing at the intri-
cate shapes and bright fish, they looked up to find that the
others were a long way away and they were alone near
a stretch of untrodden white beach. Removing their
masks and their flippers, they flopped on the sand in
the shade of a low-leaning palm.

'My God, that French piece is a bore! Thank heavens
she's not with our lot,' Roderick remarked.

Amalie said, 'She has a lovely figure.'

'And never lets anyone forget it. I've never met such a girl for arranging herself in seductive positions. The message of her body language is so loud and clear it's embarrassing.'

'It doesn't seem to embarrass Blake.'

'No, and I think Mademoiselle Hélène might be heading for trouble with him,' said Roderick. 'It could be that she's just a tease—girls who go on like that sometimes are. But if she goes on being provocative, she may find him sliding into her cabin after lights-out, then there'll be an uproar.'

'I shouldn't think Blake would do that unless he were certain of being welcome.'

It was a possibility which had not occurred to Amalie until he raised it, and it filled her with sharp distaste.

'The way she was clinging to him earlier, he could be forgiven for thinking he would be welcome,' was Roderick's reply. 'Anyway, she's not under age, and the Kingsley's can't hold it against you if he does follow up her lead.' He paused and smiled. 'Now if you were her you wouldn't be sitting there with your arms round your knees, you'd be lolling back on your elbows and smouldering at me through your eyelashes.'

'Like this?' Amalie reclined on the sand, and for a few moments burlesqued an enticing pose and expression.

He laughed. As she made to sit up, he leaned forward and, briefly, kissed her.

She gave a small sound of surprise, and he drew back and looked into her eyes. Then he kissed her again, pulling her elbows forward so that, without their support, she had to lie down.

The kiss went on for some time, but ended as gently as it had begun. Then Roderick sat up. 'I'm sorry, I've made you get sand in your hair.'

'It doesn't matter, I'll wash it out in the sea. Had we better get back?'

'Yes, perhaps we should.'

He held out a hand and pulled her up with him. When they were on their feet, he kissed her a third time, on the smooth honey curve of her shoulder.

'You're a lovely colour now,' he said. 'Living here becomes you. You were very pale when you arrived, and your eyes didn't look as green as they do now you're brown. You have very beautiful eyes. Amalie.'

She smiled, not sure how to react. There was nothing really to react to. Their embrace, and what Roderick had said, had not radically changed their relationship as a different kiss might have done. They had merely taken one step beyond ordinary friendship into the realm of affection. No decisive response was required of her. It had been an enjoyable experience, but in no way a declaration of anything but the fact that they were two young people who liked each other and who might, or might not, kiss again.

It could well have been an impulse which Roderick would never repeat. Or it might be the first of many embraces. At the moment she didn't know, and she didn't think he did either.

That night their peace was disturbed by the noise of a generator on a yacht which must have air-conditioning. Perhaps the sound was not keeping the others awake, but it irked her to the point where, if it would not have created yet more disturbance, she would have felt inclined to move the schooner to another anchorage.

Eventually, after nearly an hour's restlessness, she tried putting on the light and reading. But the book failed to hold her attention and she decided that half an hour sitting on deck in the moonlight might be more effective. Swinging her feet to the carpet, she reached for the short, cool wrapper which matched her thin cotton voile nightdress, and slid her arms into the loosely cut sleeves.

As, softly, she left her cabin and turned towards the companion-way to the deck, she glimpsed a figure ahead of her, but could not tell straight away if the woman in the filmy nightgown was Harriet or Hélène.

That it was the French girl was clear as soon as Amalie reached the deck. She could see the other's blonde hair shining under the riding light on the fore stay.

Pausing in a patch of shadow behind the mainmast, Amalie saw Blake's tall figure straighten from a leaning position as Hélène joined him at the rails.

She spoke to him, but too low for Amalie to catch the words, and in any case her own French did not compare with the idiomatic fluency with which he could speak the language, and in which he and Hélène conversed when not part of the rest of the group.

Mesmerised, Amalie watched as the French girl turned her back to the bows and leaned her forearms on the topmost rail of the pulpit, a position which flaunted her breasts, scarcely veiled by the transparent nightie.

Feeling curiously chilled, she waited for Blake to react to the unequivocal invitation expressed by Hélène's lips and body. In a moment, Amalie thought, he would lunge at Hélène as, once, he had seized hold of her; but with a very different outcome. Hélène would know how to respond to the fierce demand of his lips : she wouldn't be torn between her instincts and her inhibitions. She didn't appear to have any.

Blake was standing, half turned towards her, his fingers thrust into the pockets at the back of the jeans which were all he was wearing. It was not he who moved, but Hélène. She swayed towards him, her arms sliding up round his neck, her breasts pressed against his bare chest.

Then, to Amalie's surprise, as his hands came out of his pockets, they did not close on the French girl's sinuous waist. They moved upwards to capture her wrists and draw them down from his shoulders.

To Hélène's visible amazement—a reaction shared by Amalie—he put her firmly away from him, swung her round and gave her some low-voiced instructions which an instant later he emphasised with a single vigorous spank on the same curve which he had caressed on the day she arrived.

It was hard enough to make her yelp. No longer smiling, she flung an angry remark at him.

Blake gave her an ironic bow, before turning back to the bows to resume his midnight contemplation of the moonlit bay.

Hélène's feet were heavy on the decking as she rushed past and went below, too enraged to catch sight of the younger girl. Would the others have heard her footsteps, and wonder what was going on? Amalie wondered. Presently she followed her, moving quietly as a wraith until she regained her cabin.

There she climbed back into her bunk, and lay pondering what she had seen. She couldn't believe that Blake had rejected Hélène's advances on a matter of principle, because she was a passenger and he was employed to crew. It could only be that he didn't find her desirable, and Amalie had thought him a man who would take any pretty, willing woman who came his way. That, apparently, this was not so cast a new and less unflattering light on his rather incalculable character.

She yawned, feeling drowsy at last. Turning on her side, she closed her eyes and saw again, in her mind's eye, that unexpected rebuff. Perhaps now Hélène will turn her attention to Roderick, she thought, before sleep overcame her.

It was difficult to judge whether anyone not in the know would have noticed a change in the French girl's manner next day. By now, half way through the cruise, it seemed accepted by everyone that the two boats would stay together for the rest of the trip.

They all spent an hour of the morning looking round a colourful market, some stalls selling local produce and others wares for the tourists made from straw and shells.

'How about this one?' said Roderick, when Amalie was pausing by a stall with dozens of beach hats.

He selected a style which had rings of openwork round the crown and a wide shady brim. She put it on and studied the effect in the mirror nailed to one of the uprights which supported the awning.

'I don't think it's quite me,' she said.

'It isn't,' said Blake's voice, behind her, as she took it off. 'Try this.' He reached for a hat not unlike a Stetson but with a curlier brim, the kind of hat worn long ago by plantation owners.

'That's a man's hat,' objected Roderick.

'Men's things make some girls look more girlish,' said Blake, watching her put it on. 'Yes, that's you ... and so are these.' He reached past her and picked up a pair of large coral-red hoops from a tray of cheap ear-rings.

Standing close behind her, he held them up to her ears. Like the sweep of the hat, they did something for her.

'They're plastic, aren't they?' said Roderick, on a note of disapproval.

'Yes, but fun. I'll have them,' said Amalie.

Before she could reach in her pocket for the notes she had in it, Blake had paid for both hat and ear-rings.

'No, no, I can't let you pay, Blake.'

He shrugged. 'A few dollars? Why not?' He strolled off to look elsewhere, leaving her feeling oddly pleased and the other man wearing a frown.

'Oh, well, maybe he's right,' said Roderick. 'I don't really know much about fashion. But I should have thought one good pair of ear-rings were better than a lot of plastic junk.'

It was, she guessed, a piece of fashion philosophy picked up from his mother who was not the type to look well in the flamboyant caftans and bizarre costume jewellery which Archer Reinhardt's old mother could still carry off.

Amalie had yet to see Roderick's mother dressed up, but she guessed that classic silk shirts, plain skirts, very good quality belts and shoes, and pearls or fine antique jewels would be Lady Scott's style. Amalie herself had a foot in both camps, liking elegance sparked by occasional flashes of nonsense.

Later she wondered if the fact that Roderick had picked out the wrong hat, and Blake the right one, had any significance. Did it mean that Roderick did not see her as she really was, and Blake did? Or did it mean that Roderick was the kind of Englishman who felt clothes and furnishings were not matters which should concern his sex, whereas Blake took some interest in them?

She had a feeling that if Roderick were buying a present for a woman, it would never be luxurious underwear. But Blake, if he thought it would please her, would have no qualms about braving a lingerie department, or the nearest branch of Janet Reger whose lace and crêpe de chine nighties, and gossamer briefs and bra sets, she had often gazed at with longing.

Life must be more fun with a man who does take some interest, she thought. But was a capacity for fun an important criterion in judging someone? A man might make life amusing, yet be lacking in all the finer qualities —integrity, stability, fidelity. And without them, how long would the fun last?

That Hélène had transferred her attention to Roderick became apparent after lunch. She pursued him relentlessly for the rest of the cruise and, short of a vigorous rebuff, which clearly he felt would not do, it was difficult for him to avoid her lures.

'Oh, come, come, Roderick. No man *really* minds being waylaid by a gorgeous piece of pulchritude like Hélène,' Amalie teased him, when he complained to her that he would be glad when the trip came to an end.

'She can't actually overpower you.'

'I'm not so sure. I've never met such a man-eater. What I don't understand is why she's transferred her attentions from Blake to me.'

'Perhaps he repulsed her.'

'Perhaps tomorrow we'll have a snowstorm,' was Roderick's sceptical retort.

Amalie knew her own reaction would have been much the same had she not witnessed Blake's manner of ending Hélène's pursuit of him.

'I think it's more likely he made the pass she was asking for, and it made her sheer off in a panic,' he went on.

'Then why not try the same tactics?' Amalie suggested.

'It's not my style and, believe it or not, I'm not switched on by all that hip-swaying and lip-licking. Apart from anything else, I can't stand nails like long claws. Yours are much nicer.'

He lifted one of her hands and examined her fingernails which did not extend far beyond the tips of her fingers, and were painted with colourless varnish because she had found it impossible to keep even pale pink lacquer looking good for more than a day.

'Who gave you these?' he asked, touching the two rings she sometimes put on in the evening.

One was gold with a strap and buckle design, and the other was a gypsy ring set with a pearl and two diamonds, not very large.

'They belonged to my great-grandmother, and then Granny, whom I don't remember, wore them. I suppose the reason Grandpa didn't give them to my mother was because Victorian jewellery hadn't come into fashion in her day; and I daresay my father wouldn't have thought them suitable for her. He was already well known when they met and married, and he gave her some beautiful jewels which are Tabitha's now. But I'm very fond of these rings. Grandpa gave them to me the year he came over to see me.'

'Weren't you left any of your mother's jewels?' he asked, with a frown.

She had already discovered, from remarks made by his mother, that her grandfather seemed to have told them a good deal of the family history, including his own disapproval of his daughter's marriage to a man twenty years her senior, and about Amalie's inability to match up to her father's expectations.

'Oh, yes, I was,' she said hastily. 'My mother intended me to have her engagement ring and her watch, but of course she was wearing them when she was killed. They were never unkind to me, Roderick. It was just a terrible disappointment that I had no musical talent.'

'You have other talents, equally valuable. You make people comfortable—that's a none too common accomplishment.'

But a very mundane one, she thought, compared with Tabitha's power to draw heavenly sounds from a violoncello, and to look lovely while she was doing it, in spite of the ungraceful posture the instrument demanded.

'Tabby has the most beautiful hands you ever saw,' she said. 'Like white butterflies.'

'To be honest, I'm not too keen on cello music,' he admitted. 'Even when it's played by a top-notcher like Pablo Casals, it often reminds me of someone groaning. Amalie, there's something I want to talk to you about. I——'

But whatever it was she was not to find out that night. They were on board *Seafarer*, and just then Hélène appeared at his elbow with an ear-ring which she had dropped and stepped on. Could Roderick be clever and straighten the pin for her?

'Why not ask Blake?' he said curtly.

But Hélène was not to be fobbed off so easily, and by then Amalie felt she had been neglecting her guests for long enough, and whatever was on Roderick's mind would keep till another time.

There was a letter from Tabitha in her box at the post office when the two vessels returned to base. But Amalie had little chance to write a reply during the turn-round. With Blake busy with various minor repairs such as replacing a washer on the pump in the heads, and with routine checks on the standing and running rigging, she had her hands full with cleaning and provisioning.

The Scotts were equally busy, and it was not until their last night in port that she saw Roderick again. He came aboard after dinner and found her alone, Blake having gone ashore.

Their chores having been completed by the late afternoon, she had hoped that Blake might suggest having dinner at Marguerite's place. But in this she had been disappointed, and where he had gone after eating on board with her, or if he would reappear before bedtime, she did not know.

At first she thought Roderick had come to invite her to spend an hour on the ketch. But he did not suggest this, and half an hour later he mentioned that his mother had gone to visit her friends ashore.

Had she any notion of the result, Amalie would not have reminded him that there had been something he wanted to discuss with her, but for Hélène's intervention.

'Yes ... yes, I was coming to that. The thing is ... well, it's like this'—another pause—'Well, to be perfectly plain with you, Amalie, I think we ought to get married.'

It took her a minute or two to recover from her surprise. When she had, she said, 'We've only known each other a matter of weeks, Roderick. Isn't this rather precipitate?'

'Yes, I suppose it would be in ordinary circumstances. But we're in a situation which is somewhat extraordinary.'

'How do you mean?'

'You're dependent on Blake to keep going, and besides that you have a substantial debt hanging over you. If you sold the schooner you could not only discharge that debt, but the capital remaining would, if sensibly invested, produce quite a decent income.'

'But I should have nowhere to live.'

'You would come and live with me on *Carrageen*. At the moment I'm as dependent on Mother as you are on Blake. She never says so, but I know she would like to go back to England. She won't until I have a wife to take her place.'

'And you're suggesting we should marry because I need a crew and you need a cook?'

'Baldly—yes. But we're very well suited, you know. We've both chosen chartering as a way of life. We're of the same generation, with similar backgrounds. I'm not offering you nothing but a life of hard work. My father left me investments which allow for a fair amount of jam on the bread and butter.'

'You haven't mentioned love, Roderick.'

'No—no, I haven't.' He paused. 'That's something I can't offer, Amalie. I like you; I find you extremely attractive. But I'm not in love with you. That's over for me, I'm afraid.'

'Over?' she queried.

'Two years ago I was in love with a girl. She married someone else. I don't expect ever to feel again the way I did about Melissa and, frankly, I don't think I want to. It was a damned painful experience which it took me months to recover from.'

'I can imagine,' said Amalie. 'But should you let it affect the rest of your life? I'm not sure how old you are, but——'

'Twenty-four. Not still in my salad days.'

'No, but not beyond hoping that, next time, it will be reciprocal, surely?'

'I'm not sure that love in that sense is the soundest basis for a marriage, and I don't want to end up in the divorce court as so many people do nowadays,' said Roderick. 'Looking back, I can see quite clearly that Melissa and I weren't really right for each other. But at the time I would have married her like a shot, if she would have had me.'

'Could what you felt for her have been an infatuation rather than the real thing?'

'Maybe. But how does one tell at the time?'

'The only wise person I've ever discussed it with was Grandpa, in our letters. He——'

Again Roderick interrupted to ask, 'Have you been through it, too, then?'

'Oh, no—never.' She paused recoiling from the impact of the realisation that this was not true. She was in love at this very moment—with Blake.

'It—it was when a girl in my flat was in love with a married man, and everyone but she herself could see she was heading for heartbreak,' she went on, after a pause.

'I mentioned it in a letter, and when he wrote back Grandpa said that this was the difference between infatuation and love. Infatuation was blind to all faults and difficulties, but love saw the other person's faults and accepted them as very unlikely to be changeable. But it also took into account that no one was perfect, and to hope for perfection was to ask for disillusionment.'

'He was a sage old boy, your grandfather,' said Roderick. 'Not that I ever discussed anything of that nature with him, but one could tell that he knew one hell of a lot about human nature.'

'I remember he also warned me to remember what Balzac wrote about everyone having the defects of their qualities.'

'I don't think I quite follow that.'

His answer didn't surprise her. She had already discovered that Roderick, unlike John Lawrence, had little interest in philosophy, and none at all in poetry. His taste in books was for those written by such courageous lone voyagers as Tilman, Smeeton and Moitessier which he had read and re-read. However, when not out on charter, he preferred to spend his evenings not with a book but devising improvements to *Carrageen*, among them the red shade for the light over his chart table which enabled anyone consulting the charts after dark to retain their night vision when returning on deck.

His was of an inventive and practical nature, not much given to introspection and not, she suspected, too sensitive to other people's moods or to the more subtle nuances of social exchange.

'He meant that if a man is a strong dependable character, he's probably also rather bossy; or if a woman is essentially feminine, she won't be the sort not to turn a hair in a shipwreck,' she explained.

'I wouldn't agree with that entirely. You're a very feminine person, but I'm sure you wouldn't go to pieces in an emergency. If I thought that, I shouldn't have asked you to marry me.'

'I don't know about going to pieces. I could never, in a million years, contemplate a round-the-world voyage on my own like Dame Naomi James. If I'd had to go through what she went through in the Roaring Forties, I'm sure I'd have died of sheer terror.'

'So would most men, if it comes to that.' Rod put his arm round her shoulders. 'I don't want an intrepid wife, quite prepared to go up the mast in a rough sea if need be. I'd much rather have a good cook. You don't have to make up your mind immediately, Amalie. Think it over for a week or two. I'm sure you'll see it makes sense.'

She shook her head. 'I don't think so. It would solve some problems only to create others. I could never marry anyone unless I loved him with all my heart, and I knew he felt the same way. And you—when you've had more

time to recover from being hurt by Melissa—may yet
find a girl far more right for you than I am.'

'I doubt that. Perhaps I've been too down to earth
about this. I did say, if you remember, that I found
you very attractive.'

To prove it, he put his arms round her and kissed her.
Amalie had accepted, if not actively responded to his
other kisses. This time she found it an effort not to recoil
particularly when it turned out to be a much more ardent
embrace than any of his previous ones.

It was brought to an abrupt conclusion not by her
but a discreet cough from the top of the boarding ladder.
As they drew apart, they found Blake had returned, but
could not retire to his quarters because they were in
his way.

'Sorry to intrude,' he said. But he looked more amused
than apologetic.

'That chap is as stealthy as a cat burglar,' Roderick
said irritably, when the other man had disappeared
below.

'Yes, he's very light on his feet considering his size.
I'm sure he didn't mean to sneak up on us. It's time
I turned in, Roderick'—this as he attempted to draw her
back into his arms.

'So early?'

'I know it's not late, but I'm tired. This has been a
strenuous turn-round.'

Somewhat reluctantly he said goodnight. When he
had gone Amalie remained on deck for a time, thinking
not about Roderick's proposal, but about her discovery
that her feelings for Blake had turned full circle from
distrust to trust, from antagonism to love.

She wished he had not caught Roderick kissing her.
She foresaw that, tomorrow, he would make much mocking capital of it.

CHAPTER FIVE

In fact she did not have to wait until the morning for his teasing. When she went below he had not withdrawn to his cabin, but was in the saloon reading Chay Blyth's book, *The Impossible Voyage*, which she had sent to her grandfather the Christmas after it was published.

'My apologies for butting in on the romantic moment,' he said, as he put the book down. 'I didn't realise what was afoot until too late.'

'Nor did I the other night when I went on deck for some air and saw you and the Nicean barque at what seemed to be a romantic moment,' she answered lightly.

'The Nicean barque?' His dark brows contracted with curiosity. 'Ah, yes, I've got it—"Helen, thy beauty is to me like those Nicean barques of yore". But who wrote it, I've no idea.'

'An American—Edgar Allan Poe.'

'Really? I associate him with *Tales of Mystery and Imagination*.'

'And *Annabel Lee*, surely?'

'Yes, I'd forgotten that was his. So the Nicean barque was your nickname for our *femme fatale*?' He laughed, showing his sound white teeth. 'Had you stuck around, you'd have seen that it didn't last long, our moonlit idyll.'

'I did. She came rushing past me. I was almost as surprised as she was.'

He shrugged, his eyes still amused. 'It doesn't do for the crew to dally with the passengers. I know my place, ma'am.'

Amalie could not resist saying, 'I'm sure that wouldn't have stopped you, if you had wanted to dally. Didn't you find her attractive?'

'A little too obvious for my taste.'

'That's what Roderick said, but I thought you only discriminated agains virgins, and if Hélène was she was at great pains to disguise it.'

His blue eyes narrowed. 'Why does it rankle, Amalie, that I recognised your inexperience and stopped laying siege to you? Would you rather I'd been the type without any scruples on that score?'

'It doesn't rankle,' she answered. 'I'm just puzzled, that's all. You draw the line at seduction, and you draw the line at Hélène. What sort of girl does suit you?'

'I wonder why you're so interested?'

The sudden shrewdness of his scrutiny made her take fright and say, with a shrug, 'Oh, merely idle curiosity. Like Grandpa, I like to discover what makes people tick—and you're different from most of the people I've met.'

'Only because I'm a hybrid, and you're accustomed to thoroughbred Englishmen like Scott.'

'You always have a slight sting in your voice when you speak of him.'

'No, no—not a sting. That's envy you hear.'

'Envy? I don't believe it. Why, you're twice the man Roderick is,' she exclaimed, before she could stop herself.

'Kind of you to say so, but not true, unfortunately. I'm a good deal older than he is; years not always well spent,' he replied, on a curiously sombre note.

His forefinger keeping his place in the book, he rose. 'I'm going to turn in.' As he passed her, he paused. 'Don't think too highly of me, Amalie. I'm not a nice, clean-living, true-blue type like your Roderick.'

'He's not my Roderick.'

'He'd like to be. Goodnight.' He turned to go to his cabin.

'Don't you want a nightcap?' she asked.

Without looking back, he shook his head.

'Goodnight, Blake.'

It was not long before she followed his example. In her cabin, not feeling sleepy—she suspected he hadn't either, but had left the saloon to avoid further conversation with her—she began a letter to Tabitha, but found her thoughts straying back to Blake.

She remembered how Roderick had said of him, I feel in my bones he's a crook. She had to admit he was still something of an enigma, yet her own bones told her she could trust him. It was some time since she had bothered to lock her door at night and if, as happened occasionally, a sound disturbed her in the small hours, it no longer crossed her mind that it might be Blake coming in. In a way, she wished she did not feel so safe with him now.

Seafarer's third charter party were South Americans.

The arrangements had been made by a man called Arturo Gomez who would be accompanied by two friends, and all three by their wives—or this had been Amalie's conclusion after reading his correspondence with her grandfather.

However, as soon as the party arrived it was clear that the three female members were not the men's wives. They were flamboyant girls in their early twenties, and the men were in their late fifties.

'On this trip, we'll have our meals separately,' said Blake, on a rather grim note, when the charterers had been shown to their cabins and were unpacking.

At first Amalie attributed his tone to the fact that all six had been smoking as they came aboard; the men cigars and the girls cigarettes.

'Yes, I think that's a good idea,' she answered, with an inward smile at the thought of how Roderick's hackles would have risen had he heard the note of command in the other man's voice.

Blake's statement had been an order, not a suggestion; yet she found she did not object to being told what to do. Perhaps that was only because in this instance their minds were in accord. She might have felt some resentment had he used the same arbitrary tone about something she did not agree on.

That he had other reasons for disapproving of the new arrivals became apparent when he said, 'If you wish it, Amalie, I can get rid of them for you.'

'How can you? They have a contract.'

'A contract made with your grandfather, not with a young unmarried girl. You don't have to put up with people of this sort if you don't want to. This is your home as well as your means of livelihood, and that gives you the right to refuse hospitality to undesirables.'

'If you were to send them away, I should have to return their deposit, and refund their wasted air fares,' she told him.

His black brows contracted. 'Has the deposit been spent?'

'Oh, no, that's not a problem. Grandpa always banked all the deposits separately, and didn't touch them until the contracts had been fulfilled. But refunding the fares would be a big inroad which I could do without. And have I really any right to object to these people because I suspect them of being on an illicit fling? Some people would raise their eyebrows at my own situation —living on board with you.'

'It's not in any way comparable. Even if we were living together in the other sense, it wouldn't make you the kind of girl those three are.'

'Poor things—it's not them I dislike. It's those three horrid middle-aged lechers. I must admit if you weren't with me, I should be worried,' she conceded. 'But I'm sure you can easily handle them if they drink too much, or make any other kind of trouble. So let's go ahead and make the best of it. We needn't socialise with them, as old Mrs Reinhardt would have put it.'

Blake considered a moment, then shrugged. 'You're

the skipper,' was his answer.

'I think it might be much better if you were the skipper on this trip. I'll just be the cook,' said Amalie.

After lunch, the three men and their girls did not stay on deck to enjoy the sailing as the two previous parties had. They went below and spent the whole passage in their cabins, so that Amalie had the illusion that no one else was on board and she and Blake were on a private cruise, free to sail without plan or time-table until the breeze dropped or they happened upon an inviting anchorage.

The first of the six to reappear was one of the girls, who came on deck soon after they were at anchor. All the men spoke English; the girls did not. They spoke South American Spanish which, when Amalie asked him, Blake had said he understood.

'But it's just as well you can't,' he added. 'You wouldn't like their choice of adjectives.'

The girl who came on deck first was wearing a red bikini. Having settled herself on one of the sunbathing mattresses, she took off the top. Amalie, seeing her beginning to oil herself, without first having spread a large towel over the mattress as passengers were asked to do on the brief list of polite requests tacked to each cabin door, fetched a towel from the linen locker.

'Blake, could you explain to her that we don't want oil on the mattress?' she asked him.

The girl listened to his explanation—to Amalie's ears his command of Spanish seemed as good as his French —and stood up while he spread the towel. Then she held out her bottle of oil and said something with a smile which reminded Amalie of Hélène.

'Do you mind doing her back for her?' he asked Amalie.

'Not at all.'

As she took the bottle and he turned away, the girl added a remark which made him glance over his shoulder and return a clipped reply.

As he walked off, the girl grinned and put another question to Amalie, who indicated that she did not understand it. The girl then enquired, in sign language, if Amalie were Blake's girl. To which Amalie shook her head, and began to apply the oil.

Later she asked Blake what the girl had said to him when he had eschewed doing her back for her.

'She expressed some doubt about my virility,' he said, with a hint of amusement.

'And what did you say to her?'

'Something unfit for your ears, I'm afraid.'

'She didn't seem shocked.'

'I should think she's unshockable,' he shrugged.

'What I can't understand is why they bothered to charter us. Surely an hotel with a pool would have suited them equally well?'

'One would have thought so,' he agreed. 'But perhaps their privacy is safer with us. Gomez, Gonzalez and Lopez are three suspiciously common names; perhaps not their real ones. They may be important men who have more to lose than the good opinion of their wives.'

'One thinks how contemptible they are, and yet I suppose it must be partly their wives' fault that they're here with these girls,' she said thoughtfully.

'I doubt it. If their wives are women in their fifties, these men would have been their first lovers. Therefore it must be their own fault if their women have grown cool towards them—or were never very warm.'

'That seems an argument in favour of girls trying out various partners before they settle for one. After all, not all men can be expert lovers, and one might find oneself married to one who wasn't.'

He was splicing line round a thimble, a concave grooved metal eye, but at this he looked up and gave her a measuring glance.

'I should take a chance on that, if I were you, Amalie. I don't think experimental relationships would suit you —or prove very much.'

'I was speaking generally, not personally.'

Blake looked amused. 'Women are always speaking personally,' he said dryly.

Having their meals after the passengers had eaten made catering slightly more complicated, but was worth the extra trouble for the pleasure it gave her to be alone with him. In that sense it was the most enjoyable of the three charters.

But there were many irritations to offset this bonus. Every morning when she and Blake rose—the others rarely emerged from their sleeping quarters before mid-morning—the ash trays in the saloon would be full of cigarette ends and cigar butts left by the passengers when they had finished playing cards the night before.

One morning Amalie found a hole burned in the cover of one of the squabs, and although Blake had insisted on showing all six passengers how to operate the carbon dioxide fire extinguishers with which the schooner was well equipped, she could not help worrying a little that one of them might set fire to a mattress during the night.

All the girls sunbathed without tops, and one day Lola appeared on deck naked and was sent below by Blake on the grounds, as he explained later, that total nudity might offend passengers on boats sharing their anchorage. She and Maria were a sluttish pair whose raucous laughter grated on the ear, and who left the washroom in a mess. Amalie resigned herself to finding their pillowcases smeared with lipstick and mascara at the end of the charter.

The girl called Juanita she quite liked. She was younger and quieter than the other two. Sometimes, in repose, her face had a wistful expression.

Blake, who insisted on acting as steward when they ate and who would not allow her to serve them at all, often came back to the galley with the same grim look on his face she had seen there when he first met them.

She guessed that much of their conversation at the table was extremely coarse, and she would have been very naïve not to guess that, on the third night out, they changed partners.

'I think we should go back to base,' Blake said tersely when, for a change, he and she were the last to turn in.

Amalie knew why. She said, 'Would you turn back if you were on your own, or with another man?'

'That would be different. I'm sure your grandfather wouldn't have put up with this riff-raff.'

'I'm sure he would. It would have helped towards keeping Tabby and me in England, and that was his top priority. Mine is repaying the money he owed as fast as I can.'

'The Androcles family won't press you,' he assured her. 'The fact that you were charged interest was the fault of one of their accountants who acted off his own bat without consulting any of them.'

'Even so I'm sure Andronicus Androcles wouldn't think I should get rid of these people. Are you going to tell me he never has an orgy himself? Oh, I daresay his yacht is larger, and his girls more expensive, but is there really any difference?'

'You know nothing about him, except for some gossip you had from your lawyer.'

'No, but you must know him. Is it untrue he's a playboy? Isn't he much like these men, but on a more de luxe scale?'

'Perhaps you're right—except that he isn't their age, or married, or as undiscriminating in his choice of female companions.'

'Naturally not. He can afford the best of everything, but it doesn't make him a nicer person. Wouldn't it be rather illogical to jib at this loathsome lot when I'm up to my eyebrows in debt to someone who's very little better?'

She put her hand on his arm. 'Blake, it isn't that I don't appreciate your wish to protect me from these people—I do. I'm glad you're concerned. It shows what a nice man *you* are. But I'm not learning anything about the seamy side of life which, in theory, I didn't know already. And as long as you're looking after me, none of those men is going to make a grab at me.'

He put his hand over hers and, for an instant, she thought she saw in his eyes a softer look than any he had given her before. But almost at once it was guarded again.

'Very well, you're the skipper,' he said.

Amalie was wrong in thinking that none of the South Americans would bother her while she was under his aegis. The very next day the youngest of the three men, Lopez, came into the galley and, after some conversation, put his arm round her waist from behind.

Amalie stiffened. 'I'm very busy, Señor Lopez.'

As his mouth fastened, leech-like, on her shoulder, she gave a long shudder. But before she could wrench herself free and snatch at a stainless steel ladle with which to inflict a reprisal, his unwelcome embrace was cut short by a hard brown hand grasping his shoulder and heaving him backwards.

'Touch Miss Heron again, and you'll find yourself thrown overboard and left to swim back,' Blake told Lopez coldly, when the man, flung off balance, had lurched heavily against a worktop.

Lopez looked startled and scared. He stammered something in Spanish, and then made a bolt for it.

Blake didn't stop him. 'I've a good mind to heave the whole damned trio over the side,' he said, with angry contempt.

'Oh, you can't do that,' Amalie protested. 'But I'm

glad you stopped him. Ugh!—What a sickening man. Like a human remora'—this as, squinting sideways at her shoulder, she saw the mark left by the suction of Lopez' repulsive kiss. Another shiver ran through her.

Blake's expression changed. 'I shouldn't let it put you off. We aren't all remoras.' He bent his tall head and kissed her gently on the mouth.

It was as light a caress, if rather less brief than his first kiss; and not at all like his second. But since that night things had changed. He was no longer a stranger, and Amalie was no longer the girl she had been when they met. She had fallen in love with him.

With an instinct as old as womankind, she swayed towards him, her hands sliding up his strong arms to meet at the back of his neck. As he gripped her waist, and the first kiss merged with another, her lips parted under his, and she felt, without any alarm, the sudden fierce surge of his passion as he strained her closer against him, making her thrillingly aware of the primeval force inflamed by her eager response.

The kiss seemed to last a long time, and she wished it would go on for ever. His hands, roving over her back, sent ripples of pleasure down her spine. Her bikini which, with the other man, had seemed such a scanty defence against the detestable familiarities she had felt he was capable of attempting, now seemed to cover too much of her. She would not have minded where Blake touched her and wished they were somewhere more private where he need not restrict his caresses.

Just how much she had changed from the girl he had kissed on the landing stage, and how few inhibitions she had left, was brought home to her when the kiss ended.

As she opened her eyes he looked down at her and said dryly, 'How long is it since we last did this? Not much more than a month ago, surely? Either Scott must be a better tutor than one would suppose, or you must be a very quick pupil.'

His tone brought a quick flush of colour into her cheeks. 'Roderick didn't kiss me the second time we met, or the way you did that night.'

He lifted an eyebrow. 'No?'

'No—never.'

'More fool he,' was Blake's derisive comment. 'If he had, he might have come in for this outbreak of eager libido which he, presumably, triggered. I seem to recall a much more maidenly reaction the last time I kissed you.'

His hands were still on her hips, and she could not step back because the sink was behind her. She put her hands on his wrists to free herself, and he let his arms fall to his sides. But he did not step back and, with only inches between them, she was still in the field of his magnetism.

'If you will pounce on people so precipitately, you can't expect always to be welcome,' she answered, trying to sound self-possessed, although her heart was still pounding.

The vivid blue eyes were mocking. 'I didn't expect to be quite so welcome this time. Better watch it, Mis' Amalie honey. If you let yourself go like that with Scott, he might lose his head, poor devil. Sometimes those thoroughly decent, upright Englishmen can become as lecherous as Lopez ... or a half-Greek wastrel like me.'

'I never called you a wastrel. I felt you were wasted as a bodyguard. And I shan't ever let myself go, as you put it, with Roderick. He's asked me to marry him, and I've refused him.'

'It seems I'm not the only one inclined to be too precipitate. A proposal as soon as this—the lad must be crazy.'

'It was you who forecast that he would.'

'Yes, but not for three or four months,' said Blake. 'I should think his knowledge of women is about as strong as mine of horses. He certainly can't know you well.'

'But you feel you do, I suppose?'

'I've just spent three weeks in considerably closer proximity to you than he has—and I've kissed you more thoroughly, you tell me. But I shouldn't at this stage, feel we were ready to commit ourselves to spending the rest of our lives together.'

'You aren't the marrying kind; Roderick is. He wants a wife.'

'Urgently!' Blake said flippantly.

Amalie felt hurt that, following an embrace which had stirred her to the roots of her being, he seemed so little affected. She had hoped for some sign of tenderness, but there had been more gentleness in his voice when he had said *We're not all remoras* than there was now.

'I think you were right to refuse him at this early stage. You may change your mind later on. You could do a lot worse,' Blake went on.

'And a lot better. I don't—could never—love Roderick.'

'Because his kisses aren't as arousing as mine? Practice makes perfect. He'll learn how you like to be kissed if you give him the chance.'

She stepped sideways, edging away. 'You're talking about sex. I was talking about love, which is being the same kind of people, wanting the same kind of life.'

'You are, and you do, I should have thought.'

She shook her head. 'No, not really. There are all kinds of little differences. Roderick may have opted out of a conventional career himself, but he would feel—he's said so—that his sons must be educated at English schools: boarding schools. I was never terribly close to my parents, but I'd hope for a much closer relationship with my children, and I couldn't bear them to be sent away at eight, or even at thirteen.'

'No, I agree with you there. I'd hate to think a son of mine was being held by the legs with his head in the lavatory and the chain pulled by one of the bullies who exist in every boys' school.'

'That didn't happen to you, did it?' she exclaimed in horror.

'No, and it wouldn't have worried me if it had. I should have held my breath. But I've known it done to other boys—and not intervened, I regret to say.'

'If you had the bullies would have turned on you.'

'I doubt it—I was always tall for my age. But a communal life doesn't make for civilised attitudes. Anyway I shouldn't have thought Scott would be able to afford to educate his sons in England. Or has he some private means in addition to his charter income?'

'Yes, I believe so.'

'And that has no influence on you?'

'It's the very *last* thing which would influence me. Would you marry Stella Androcles if she asked you?'

Slightly to her surprise, his reply was an immediate and emphatic, 'God forbid!'

'She's much, much richer than Roderick will ever be.'

'It's a different matter for a man to marry a rich woman. People call him her lapdog. No particular odium attaches to a woman who marries a rich man, or only if the discrepancy between their ages is a very wide one.' He eyed her thoughtfully for a moment. 'Wouldn't you like some emerald ear-rings to bring out the green in your eyes, and a red fox fur coat—or whatever is in at the moment—to wear when you visit your sister?'

'Tabitha would adore a red fox coat—and she'll probably have one, one of these days. The only jewel I've ever seen which did rather tempt me—or which would have, if I'd had the money—was a very large opal in quite a plain gold setting but cut in the form of a scarab.'

'Sounds unusual,' he commented. 'Where did you see it?'

'In the window of a jeweller in Bond Street. Philip Antrobus I think it was. If I'd had Tabby with me that day, she'd have sailed in and asked the price—as if she were a millionairess,' said Amalie, smiling to herself at the memory of some of her sister's more audacious actions. 'But they'd know at a glance that I wasn't.'

'You may yet be. The West Indies are full of rich men.'

'All middle-aged, if not old. I'd rather be a young man's slave, thanks. I'd better get on with the supper.'

Later that afternoon Amalie had a conversation with Roderick over the radio-telephone. It was an arrangement they had made before leaving harbour and she was in her grandfather's quarters, waiting for his call when it came through.

Aware that their conversation was not private—there might be others listening in on the same frequency—Amalie had to be guarded when he asked her how things were going.

'Not as well as last time, or the time before. But there's nothing to worry about. I might be in difficulties on my own, but there are no problems which the watch on deck can't handle,' was her discreet reply.

'I hope you're right,' said Roderick. 'By the way, do you remember us talking not long ago about a chap who told you he'd been to Winchester? I thought it might interest you to know that I've found out since that he hadn't. I remembered afterwards that I knew someone who had and, out of curiosity, I asked him to check. No one of that name had been there for five years either side of the relevant period. It shows I wasn't far wrong when I told you I thought the chap was a bit of a con merchant, doesn't it?'

Amalie received this dismaying information with a protracted silence which made Roderick think she might have gone off the air. When he had checked that she was still receiving him, she said, 'Are you sure your information is reliable?'

'One hundred per cent. Someone should tax him with

it, and make him realise not everyone is as gullible as he seems to think.'

'I don't think there would be much point in that, Roderick. To tell that kind of untruth is not the same as misleading people for gain. What would be the point of embarrassing him?'

'His ego could stand being deflated, if you ask me. I thought him too damned sure of himself. I know Mother liked him, but she's as susceptible to charm as any other woman. Myself, I can't stand a liar.'

'Nor can I, in the ordinary way,' she answered. 'But in this particular case I can hardly believe it was a lie. He just doesn't ... didn't seem the type to go in for false pretences of that nature.'

'It shows one can never be too careful with people one doesn't know well. Not that you've known us for long, but your grandfather had. Anyway, I thought it would be as well to put you on your guard. If you should run into him again, don't forget that under his winning ways there's a shifty streak and perhaps some other unpleasant traits besides a disregard for the truth.'

When the call was over Amalie remained where she was, pondering Roderick's indictment of the man to whom, did the younger man but know it, she had already given her heart.

Perhaps the blow would have been worse had she not already had reason to know that Blake was no angel. Had she thought him perfect, Roderick's information would have come as an even more unpleasant surprise. But life had already taught her that very few people came near perfection, least of all herself with her childhood jealousy—overcome long ago—of her sister's superior place in their parents' affections.

That night, some time in the small hours, she was jerked out of sleep, knowing at once that something was wrong, but not what it was. It took perhaps fifteen seconds be-

fore she realised the sounds which had roused her were
the engine and the powered windlass hauling the anchor
cable up through the hawse pipe.

Not pausing to put on either slippers or a wrap,
Amalie rushed on deck to find, with a surge of relief, that
it was Blake who was responsible for her awakening.
She had been afraid it might be one of the others indulg-
ing in a tipsy whim to test the schooner's motor power.

'What's happened?' she asked.

'There's been a Mayday—a fire on the yacht *Poseidon*.
Four adults, four children on board. No one else
acknowledged the call. We should reach her in thirty
minutes.'

'Oh, God!' Her low exclamation expressed every seafarer's fear of the terrible swiftness with which a vessel
could burn out, leaving all on board—if there had been
time to escape—at the mercy of the treacherous ocean.
Even here, in these warm latitudes, a night adrift in a
life-raft could be a fearful ordeal, especially for anyone
with burns.

Blake had already brought inboard the boarding ladder, and moved the dinghy astern. Now, together, they
furled the awning. By now they had done it so often it
had become a fine art which, if they exerted themselves,
they could do very quickly indeed. Then, with the anchor
at home and the engine warmed up, he switched to full
power.

Amalie went below to dress. As she was leaving her
cabin for the second time, Señor Gomez emerged from
his quarters.

He addressed her in irritable Spanish, forgetting she
could not speak it. Switching to English, he demanded
to know what was going on.

'We have to go to the aid of another yacht which is in
trouble, but we shan't reach her for half an hour. There's
nothing you can do to help at present, señor,' she told
him.

'By what right do you disturb my sleep? I have chartered this ship and it is for me to give the orders. I cannot rest with so much noise.'

Amalie said very politely, 'If you refer to your contract, you will see that the charterer must abide by the Captain's decision in all nautical matters. Captain Blake wouldn't ignore a distress signal if the Queen of England were on board.'

She made for the hatch, and he followed her, protesting and complaining.

By now they were clear of the bay, and on their course north.

Blake said, 'Take over here, would you, Amalie? I've one or two things to do below.'

As she moved to take over the helm, the short, paunchy South American clothed in his gaudy silk dressing-gown began to address his complaints to the tall man in sun-faded jeans but otherwise naked.

Both men had a dark growth of beard, but Blake's small hours' stubble was a shadow on lean cheeks and a strong chin. The other man's facial bones were lost under the heavy jowls of the glutton. In the upward glow from the binnacle all their features were in marked contrast. Gomez had full purplish lips, always moist, and slack in repose. Blake's mouth reflected his moods, sometimes having a humorous quirk, sometimes a hint of sensuality, and now, as he listened to Gomez, taking on the hard set of impatience.

He let the South American rant for a minute or two, and then, without raising his voice, but in a tone she had never heard from him before, and which was extraordinarily menacing, he said, 'You stupid bastard! Don't you care that children are in danger? Go back to your cabin and stay there. Get dressed and wait for my orders. Otherwise keep out of my way.'

He made a slight forward movement which sent Gomez scuttling for the hatch.

'*Christos!* What scum they are,' Blake muttered, in a milder tone.

'He thought you were going to hit him. So did I for a minute.'

'What? Thump a craven little rat half my size? Hardly,' was his dry response.

When he had left her, Amalie did not think about the repercussions of what had just happened. Her only concern was to reach *Poseidon* as fast as possible.

Blake was gone for about ten minutes. When he came back, she thought he would take over the wheel, but, having peered over her shoulder at the compass, he said, 'If you're okay here, I'll get back on the radio and try to relay *Poseidon*'s message to a shore station. I've already run through the directions for first aid for burns in your *Yachtsman's Doctor*, but the nearest hospital is at least three hours from *Poseidon*'s position and, if anyone is very badly burned, we have to consider getting professional help to them a hell of a lot faster than that.'

It was easy, on so calm a night, to keep the schooner steady on her course. Amalie wondered what they would find when they reached the scene of the disaster. She was thankful she had Blake with her, generating calm and confidence as surely as the engine provided power to fall back on should the wind fail when speed was vital.

She could never have suppressed Gomez with those brief incisive orders delivered in a tone which had made even her flinch a little.

He was a formidable man, Blake, and not only because of his physical strength. It had seemed to her that, in those moments, he had emanated an authority far greater than that of any ordinary strong arm man. The role of captain seemed natural to him; responsibility rested as lightly on his broad shoulders as it weighed heavily on hers. She knew she was not a natural leader. Her role, as perhaps of most women, was to be the efficient aide-de-camp, not without resource or initiative, but lacking the inborn power to command respect and obedience, except in young children.

Thinking on these lines, she knew that, when this emergency was over, and she had a chance to talk privately to him, she was going to ask him to take command of the schooner on a more permanent basis. And, if he brought up the subject, to admit she had fallen in love with him, and was his for as long as they could be happy together—which, on her side, would be forever.

But this last she wouldn't admit because he might find it oppressive.

Poseidon when they reached her had neither sunk nor had she been reduced to a floating hulk. The two men on board had managed to put out the fire, but not before it had wrecked the saloon and the galley. Neither man had been seriously burned, and the women and children had abandoned the yacht at the outset, taking refuge on the nearest beach and going through a bad half an hour for fear there might be an explosion while the men were on board.

Their chief anxiety when Blake and Amalie put ashore was not the damage to the yacht but the condition of one of the wives. She was seven months pregnant, and the shock of the fire had brought on pains which suggested a premature labour.

'It's a pity Reinhardt and Kingsley aren't with us this week,' said Blake, when they were all aboard *Seafarer*. 'No doubt there are midwives on several islands hereabouts, but how soon may she give birth? And how risky is a birth which starts two months too soon?'

'I don't know. Perhaps not too risky for the mother, if she's had other babies before, but this one may be very small and in need of an incubator.'

'We can probably rig up a makeshift good enough to serve for a few hours.'

His imperturbable sang-froid undisturbed even by this

contingency, Blake turned to the *Yachtsman's Doctor* which included a section on childbirth.

By this time the pregnant woman had been put to rest in Amalie's cabin, with her worried husband in attendance. The second wife and her husband were engaged in putting all four children to bed in Blake's twin-bunk cabin. She had no helpful advice to offer. She herself was upset and tearful, and unfit to cope with any more strain.

'I shall just have to manage as best I can. I've seen a film of a birth, so I know roughly what to expect and what has to be done,' said Amalie, hoping she sounded more resolute than she felt.

His hidden smile was full of warmth. 'That's my girl!' he said, with approval.

Suddenly all she wanted from life was to be Blake's girl—better, his woman. Together, what could they not do?

> *For I,*
> *Except you enthrall me, never shall be free,*
> *Nor ever chaste, except you ravish me.*

She remembered the words of the poem she had been reading on the day, nearly three weeks ago, when Blake had appeared on the quay and told her he was her crew.

No wonder the lines had seemed to have a special meaning for her. She had known, even then, how easily Blake could enthrall her.

As he had.

The poem, slightly puzzling when she had read it, was all at once totally clear. Only the state of being forever enthralled by one man made a woman free of the life-long searching for love which bedevilled so many lives. And only by total subjection to one fiercely demanding lover could it become impossible for her ever to want any other man.

'We'll manage together,' said Blake.

But in the event, they didn't have to. Help came from

an unexpected quarter. The girl called Juanita heard what was happening, and she took charge of the situation, having had, as she told him, much experience. Had not her own mother given birth to a child every year of Juanita's life until, at fourteen, she had left home, such as it was, to make her own way in the world?

A baby boy, by no means as small as they had anticipated—either his mother had miscalculated or he would have been very large if born at full term—made his entrance into the world less than fifteen minutes before they berthed at an island with good medical facilities.

An ambulance, and a doctor, were awaiting their arrival on the quay, and very soon mother and child had been transferred into professional care, and the rest of *Poseidon*'s people had departed to find rooms in an hotel. Blake went with them as neither of the men seemed competent to cope with the situation in which they found themselves.

It had emerged, during the night, that neither family had any previous sailing experience. Their previous holidays had always been organised package deals. They had rented *Poseidon*, a bareboat, through an advertisement in a newspaper. From Blake's and Amalie's point of view, it was hard to decide who was the more irresponsible, the yacht's owners or the two men who had failed to realise the hazards of such a holiday.

If she had been able to converse with her Amalie would have tried to find out why Juanita could not break free of the life she had been forced into by being born, so Blake had learned, in a shanty town slum on the fringe of a world-famous city. The girl had a natural talent for nursing, but probably her lack of education would preclude her from making use of it fully. Her plight made Amalie thankful to have been born in circumstances where literacy was taken for granted.

Without Blake to interpret for them, the two girls could only share a toasted sandwich and several cups of hot coffee. Presently Juanita went to bed, and Amalie, too, was half asleep in the saloon when Blake returned.

He sent her to bed, agreeing to wake her in time to cook the charterers' late breakfast.

She was woken by someone shaking her, and opened her eyes to find him bending over her bunk.

'What time is it?' she asked sleepily.

'Lunch time.'

'*Lunch time!*' Amalie jerked into a sitting position. 'Why didn't you wake me when you said you would?'

'Because you were exhausted. You had less than four hours' sleep last night.'

'So did you. You must be dead on your feet.'

'No, I've also had a short nap. An hour, but enough to refresh me, and I had a hot shower after mine, as I suggest you do now. By the time you're ready, lunch will be ready. We're having gammon steaks with pineapple.'

'Cooked by whom? One of the girls?'

'Cooked by me. The girls and their escorts are no longer with us. By a fortunate chance the inter-island plane was not even half full this morning, so I put them on it.'

'They've gone? I don't understand,' Amalie exclaimed bewilderedly.

'I felt that—with the possible exception of Juanita—they'd outstayed their welcome,' he answered. 'But there's no need for you to worry about having to compensate them for the few days they've lost. There'll be no question of them sueing you for breach of contract. I suspect the whole trip is being paid for out of public funds, so they're not going to make a fuss over this slight curtailment.'

He paused before adding, with a smile, 'I think it will be rather pleasant to do as we please for a day or two before returning to base. There was a time when you might have had reservations about sailing anywhere alone with me, but I don't think you feel that way now, do you?'

She wasn't quite sure what he meant by this, but it didn't matter because she *was* sure of her love for him.

'I can't think of anything nicer—especially after this charter which has been so extremely *un*enjoyable.'

'Good,' was his brisk comment. 'Now off you go to have your shower or the steaks will be overdone.'

With the steaks, they drank chilled champagne.

'A bottle I *bought*,' he remarked, when Amalie came on deck to find a table for two laid under the awning, and Blake peeling off the gold foil on a bottle very like the two he had filched from the cellars at Paradise.

After lunch, he said, 'Where shall we go? Let's look at the charts.'

'Anywhere ... anywhere,' said Amalie lazily.

She was happy to be rid of the South Americans; happier to have three days' holiday; happiest of all to be spending them alone with this most exciting of men.

'You wouldn't be the slightest bit tiddly, would you?' he asked her, raising an eyebrow.

'I don't think so.' But perhaps she was for what she would have liked to happen next was to be picked up in his arms, and carried below and made a woman ... his woman.

Blake seemed not to sense her mood. He said, 'I think an early night is indicated, after our short sleep last night. Come on, let's wash up and get going.'

When, presently, they left the harbour, she decided his judgment was better than hers. A secluded and moonlit anchorage off an uninhabited island would be a more pleasing setting for the start of an unofficial honeymoon than a curtained cabin infiltrated by all the 'noises off' a crowded port.

But their first night alone, at sea, did not turn out as she expected.

After swimming, they drank Euphoria, a French-island

drink made from two parts of rum and grapefruit juice to one each of Curaçao and pineapple juice, stirred with ice. By which time potatoes, put to bake in the oven, were ready to eat with salami and salad.

Before supper was over Amalie found lack of sleep beginning to catch up with her again. Try as she would she could not fight off her drowsiness.

'Bed time for you, I think, Skipper,' said Blake, as she swallowed a yawn.

'I'm sorry. I should be much less tired than you are.'

'I am tired now. We'll both feel more on form tomorrow. We'll stay where we are and relax, shall we?'

'I think that's a splendid idea—a whole lovely day with nothing to do but enjoy ourselves.' She clenched her teeth against another huge yawn. 'I'll leave the dishes until the morning.'

'Yes, do that.' As she rose from the table, he stood up and reached for her hand. His lips brushed lightly over her knuckles. 'Goodnight.'

'Goodnight, Blake.'

With mingled regret and relief—for still, deep down, there was a part of her which drew back from surrendering herself to him utterly without some commitment on his side—she went to the washroom to brush her teeth, and then to her cabin where she tumbled into her bunk like a weary child and, within minutes, was asleep.

She woke at sunrise, all the strains of the South Americans' charter and the fatigue resulting from their last night on board, washed away by her long, deep sleep.

Eager to begin the day, and no longer made cowardly by tiredness, she bounced out of bed and saw bright eyes and smiling lips reflected in the mirror as she brushed her hair. To celebrate this special day she put on an unworn bikini of velvety apricot towelling.

Presently, going to the galley, she found the sink empty, the supper dishes put away. She put on coffee, then stepped on deck to see if Blake might be in the water although, had he been swimming, she would have expected to find the coffee already on.

He was nowhere to be seen. On impulse, Amalie went to his cabin, tapped on the door and, when there was no response from within, quietly opened it a few inches.

He was still sleeping, lying on his back with the upper part of his face hidden by an upflung forearm and a sheet drawn loosely over him, covering his legs and hips.

Amalie stepped over the coaming and advanced into the cabin. As Blake had woken her up the day before, she laid her hand on his bare shoulder, and softly repeated his name until he moved his arm and she saw that his eyes were open. One moment he had been asleep; the next he seemed fully alert, smiling at her.

'It's a perfect morning. I thought you wouldn't want to waste any of it.'

He didn't answer, but reached out his arm to encircle her hips and draw her down to him. She would have yielded, but suddenly he put his other hand up to his jaw which rasped when he rubbed it.

He grimaced, and released her. 'I'll join you as soon as I've shaved.'

She nodded and turned away, guessing that he was naked under the sheet, and unable to help feeling some shyness. But to feel shy was not the same as being doubtful, and her last doubts had gone in the night. Now it was day, and she felt a joyous conviction that to love Blake without reservation, and to let him make love to her, could only enrich her life and be something she would be glad to remember when she was old. Her decision was made, irreversibly; now all that remained was for him to choose the right moment to take her in his arms.

It was during breakfast that she remembered to ask him something which had been at the back of her mind for thirty-six hours.

'Blake, how was it you heard the Mayday? I ought to have heard the alarm signal, being near to the radio cabin, but I shouldn't have thought you would have heard it from yours.'

'I was in the radio cabin, preparing to make a telephone call.'

'A telephone call! At that hour?'

'Two o'clock in the morning here is breakfast time elsewhere,' he answered. 'Don't worry, I'll pay for all my calls, although that one was never made. The Mayday intervened.'

They spent most of the morning swimming, before going ashore with the cool boxes for a picnic lunch on the beach.

Since drawing her to him in his cabin, and then releasing her again, Blake had made no move to advance their relationship. Amalie began to wonder if, having once gone too far and too fast for her, this time he was waiting for her to give him a lead.

They had shared a bottle of wine, and a bottle of ice-cold water, and he was lying flat on his back with his hands clasped under his head, when she ventured to say, 'Blake, are you sleepy, or can I talk to you?'

His eyes remained closed, but his voice sounded fully awake as he said, 'Talk away.'

'Our first two charters ... I think you enjoyed them, didn't you?'

'Very much. It's not what one would call a hard life, this.'

'It isn't always plain sailing, as we've discovered this week. But I think it's a healthy life, never dull or monotonous, and if, after four or five years, one grows tired of cruising the same seas, one can move without losing all one's business. When my grandfather moved from the Mediterranean, any number of his previous customers followed him out here. Anyway, what I'm leading up to is the question of whether you might like to become *Seafarer*'s skipper in reality as well as appearance? I'm offering you a partnership.'

At this he did open his eyes and raise himself on his elbows. 'What kind of partnership, Amalie?'

'A complete one. A half share in the schooner, and half the profits.' She found herself unable to look at him as she added the third condition, and she swivelled herself to face the sea before saying, 'And me as well.'

Out of the corner of her eye, she saw him jerk into a sitting position. 'You as well?' he said questioningly.

'Most of the charterers seem to conclude we're lovers, and don't seem to disapprove greatly. So as I ... I've grown very fond of you, and I think you like me a little, it seems a natural concomitant to a working partnership.'

She felt his hand on her back, first at the nape of her neck, and then sliding slowly down between her shoulder-blades, past the bowtied cords of her bikini top and down to the small of her back where it stopped, and he said, 'I like you more than a little, Amalie. You're a nice girl—in every sense.'

'Then ... you accept?'—turning to him.

His palm left her back. He shook his head. 'No, I can't.'

'But why not?'

'You remember our conversation in the galley the other day, after Lopez made a nuisance of himself?'

'After you kissed me—yes, I remember.'

'If it's too soon for Scott to ask you to marry him, it's much too soon for you to propose a liaison of that sort with me. You know almost nothing about me.'

'I know all that's necessary. On the working side, you couldn't be better; and on the personal side ... well, I know all a woman needs to know. You're very clean. You have no off-putting habits. You read. You aren't ever boring. When you kiss me, I flip, as they say.' She was trying not to sound too intense. 'Surely those are the really important things.'

'For a woman—yes, very possibly. But you're still a green girl, my dear.'

'I'm still a virgin. That doesn't make me a half-wit. I did spend nearly two years in London, and I met quite a number of men, not all of them the soul of chivalry. One or two were rather unpleasant, to put it mildly.'

Blake did not reply for some moments, but sat with his elbows balanced on his updrawn knees, his longer fingers interlaced, and his thumbs pressed against the square, jutting bone of his chin.

At length, and with obvious reluctance, he said, 'I haven't been altogether straight with you, Amalie.'

She said calmly, 'I know you haven't.'

'You know?' His expression was suddenly wary.

'It's very true, that old Biblical saying—Be sure your sins will find you out. But I don't count a little false boasting as a very black sin. Almost everyone does it at times.'

'Boasting?'

'Saying you were an old Wykehamist when you're not.'

It was hard to read his reaction to being confronted with the lie. As before, when she had said bluntly that taking champagne from the cellars at Paradise was tantamount to theft, he did not seem greatly embarrassed. But having told her he was not in the habit of lying, she had thought that, this time, he would show more discomfiture.

After a pause, he asked, 'What makes you say that?'

'Roderick found out. I mentioned it to him—I forget in what context—and he didn't believe it. Perhaps he sensed that I liked you better than him, and it made him jealous and suspicious. Anyway, it seems that someone he knows *is* an old Wykehamist, and Roderick asked him to check on you. There was no one named Blake at Winchester during the years when you would have been there. A really efficient con man would have checked that himself,' she added lightly.

'I see. And this revelation hasn't put you off me?'

She met his eyes, and said frankly, 'I don't think anything could do that now, Blake.' Having thus completely exposed the depth of her feeling for him, she hurried on. 'To quote the Bible again—which shows that the school chaplain's sermons didn't always fall on deaf ears—"He that is without sin, let him cast the first stone." I'm no angel of goodness myself. Anyway, it's the motive for a lie which is important, and if I'm right about your motive, it's a very forgivable one.'

His elbows were still on his knees, but his head had sunk forward so that his face was hidden from her. His hands were spread over his skull, the fingers plunged into the thick close cap of his hair.

It was an attitude suggestive of various reactions. He might be racking his brain for a way to excuse himself. He might be furious at being found out. He might be recalling other lies he had told, and feeling ashamed of himself and his whole way of life.

'What do you think my motive was?' he asked her, without looking up.

'From the little you told me about your background, I had the impression your childhood couldn't have been a very happy one. Maybe you always felt an outsider in both worlds. When children aren't made to feel valuable, they often invent a fantasy world which makes up for the deficiencies of their real world. At one time I used to make believe I was an even greater prodigy than Tabitha. My instrument was the harp. Sometimes people don't outgrow their fantasies. I can't remember if you'd met Roderick at the time you told me about Winchester; but if it was after meeting him, perhaps it was a reaction to the fact that he'd had all the things you lacked—distinguished father, gracious mother, public school, Oxbridge and so on.'

Blake raised his head and met her eyes. 'I called you a green girl, but you're very wise in some ways. You make allowances for people. You don't seem to have the intolerance which is usual at your age.'

'One doesn't have to make allowances for you, Blake. Ever since you've been crewing for me, I've realised you're a born captain. You have the kind of natural authority which the man in command has to have to make the passengers feel safe, and to put down trouble-makers like Gomez.'

She laid her hand on his upper arm where, even when he was relaxed, a powerful bicep made a convex curve under the taut brown skin. 'So will you accept my proposition?'

He put a hand over hers. 'I wish I could, but it isn't possible. There are reasons why I can't stay in the Caribbean indefinitely. I have ... responsibilities in Europe.'

For the first time, with consternation, Amalie wondered if he might be married. 'Not a wife?—Not children?'

'No, nothing like that. But, among other things, my mother is not very well now, and she likes to see me fairly often.'

She slipped her hand free. 'Is ... is that the only reason?'

He said, almost roughly, 'You can't be in any doubt that I want you: more now that when I first saw you.'

Amalie's lashes had been lowered. Now she lifted them, no longer caring what he read in her eyes, only conscious of time running out for them.

'Kiss me again, Blake,' she whispered.

For a second or two he didn't move. When he did, it was with the suddenness and swiftness with which he had plucked her out of the dinghy after their first dinner date.

One instant she was sitting looking at him with long-ing eyes and parted lips. The next she was lying on her back, locked in a passionate embrace, his mouth on her eyelids, her throat, her shoulders, the swell of her breasts where her suntan merged with a narrow margin of paler skin, sometimes covered and sometimes not according to the cut of her bikinis, and then, as he was discovering, with the skin which was her natural colour, not white but a pearly cream until it changed to soft pink and his questing lips drew a purr of ecstasy from her.

'Oh, darling ... darling,' she breathed, her fingers in his thick hair, her body arching with pleasure.

Then he kissed her impatient mouth while his hands caressed her to unbelievable delight which, all at once, stopped when he groaned, 'Oh, God! What the hell am I doing?' and wrenched himself free of the arms she had wound round his neck.

'You make me behave as if I were the same age as you,' he said, with savage self-contempt, as he sprang to his feet and strode away, into the sea.

Amalie lay where he left her until the storm of feeling had subsided a little. Then, slowly, she sat up and saw Blake, now several hundred yards away, cutting through the water with a fast crawl, as if he were racing.

Why had he gone like that? she wondered. Because of his scruples about virgins? Referring to his mother's indifferent health, he had said 'among other things'. What other things? Although he had seemed to blame himself for the feverish kisses they had exchanged, when his blood had cooled would he think less of her for allowing him so much licence?

These, and other unanswerable questions, flitted through her mind as she watched him swim far away and then return at the same punishing speed.

When he came out of the water he was breathing hard, but not panting as most men would have been after ten minutes of similar exertion. The outlines of his ribs showed under the darkly tanned skin each time his lungs expanded. Water coursed down his sinewy thighs. He was built as beautifully as a racehorse or a leopard, with only muscle under his skin and no fat to blur the fine proportions of his frame.

A man, but made like a god, she thought, her pulses

quickening again as he came towards her.

'Start packing up, will you? We're going back to base,' he said decisively.

'Now? At once?'

He nodded.

'Why, Blake?'

'Because I can't trust myself when I'm alone with you, Amalie. And the arrangement you suggested earlier isn't right for you. You may think you'd be happy, but you wouldn't. No, don't argue with me. I know—and I'm not proud of it—more about the lasting power of sexual attraction than you, I hope, will ever know. Without other forms of rapport between the two people involved, it has *no* lasting power. Six months is about its limit.'

'Even six months of happiness is not to be sneezed at,' she answered.

'But you wouldn't be happy—that's the point. And I shouldn't enjoy myself either, knowing you were being hurt.'

'Is that all there is between us? Sex? Nothing else?'

'I didn't say that. But, to be permanent, happiness depends on a great many factors including the right environment and satisfactory occupations. You've found your place here. Mine is elsewhere.'

She could see that, in his present mood, Blake was not to be budged; and indeed the existence of an infirm mother did seem an insuperable obstacle to his taking command of *Seafarer*.

'Your mother wouldn't be happy living on board with you, as Angela Scott does?' she asked tentatively.

He shook his head. 'My mother's natural milieu is as different from this as Lady Scott's.' He picked up the cool box and carried it back to the dinghy.

Amalie stood up and shook out the sand-mat on which she had been sitting. His mother would be younger than Roderick's mother, presumably. But even if she had been a mere girl when Blake was born, and was now barely fifty, probably a Greek peasant woman of that age would look years older than her contemporaries in northern Europe, especially if she were not well. Amalie visualised his mother as small and prematurely lined, perhaps always dressed in black with a cloth over her hair, and work-worn hands.

Less than two hours after the blissful but all too brief interlude in Blake's arms, Amalie found herself at the helm, with the genoa jib set in place of their usual headsail in order to increase their speed.

Presently Blake took over and she went below to prepare their supper which she had expected to have in the peaceful seclusion of their last anchorage, but which now seemed likely to be a hurried meal, eaten in silence.

Apart from a few terse instructions he had not spoken to her since they came back on board, making her regret that she had precipitated the emotional crisis between them of which this was the unexpected backlash.

Had she not done so, they might still be on friendly terms, instead of racing back to base. And when they reached it? What then? she wondered unhappily. He had promised to give her a fortnight's notice before leaving, but he might feel now that he could waive it. On the other hand, he wouldn't leave her crewless, of that she felt sure.

As she dried a lettuce in the salad-spinner, she remembered his statement that environment was an important part of happiness, and how she herself had told him, not long ago, that this was her place in the world, and she could never leave it.

Only for him. With him, she could be happy anywhere. What if *Seafarer* were to return to the Mediterranean, to charter among the Greek islands where his mother lived?

But the same idea must have crossed Blake's mind, particularly as she had remarked, only that afternoon, that a charter boat was not confined to any one area, and that John Lawrence had come here from the Mediterranean.

If he wanted her, in the fullest sense, he would have suggested that solution. But clearly, on his side, the pull between them was not strong enough: she was just one more girl whom he wanted to bed but not wed.

At supper he said, 'When we get back, we'll go to Paradise and put a call through to Greece to see if Adelpho is free now to come over and crew for you for the rest of the season. If not, there will be someone else. *This* arrangement has outlived its practicability. I was a fool to think it wouldn't.'

'Won't you miss it—this life you've led for the past three weeks?' she asked him.

'Yes, I shall miss it—and you. These three weeks have been more of a change for me than you realise.'

Amalie felt impelled to ask, 'If it hadn't been for your mother, would you have considered accepting the business partnership?'

He had almost finished eating. Amalie had scarcely begun her fish salad. She had no appetite for it.

Blake said bluntly, 'No,' and seemed to be going to leave it at that. But, after a pause, he went on, 'Such a partnership might be possible between two much older people, but not between us—or any other man and girl who found each other attractive and were going to live on the job, in the closest propinquity. But apart from that aspect of it, and much as I've enjoyed three weeks of the simple life, it wouldn't content me indefinitely. I like cities too. Given a choice between this and London or Paris, I'd have to choose one of the capitals. This is a fine life, Amalie, but not for me—or not yet. I'm sorry.'

She lifted a nonchalant shoulder, her throat tight with unshed tears. 'Never mind. It's ... just one of those things.'

'No, it isn't,' he said, on a harsh note. 'It's bad luck—damnable bad luck.' He got up, and went back on deck.

Later the wind dropped, but they pressed on under power. Blake took the first of the three night watches, calling Amalie at midnight for the middle watch, and taking over at four a.m. for the morning watch. When he roused her again they were nearly there.

The berth they had left was still free, but the vessel to starboard had gone, and a new boat had taken its place. Having berthed, they put covers over the furled sails; the roller-furled jib had its own built-in cover sewn down the leech and along the foot.

They were rigging the awning when a voice cried, 'Andro! Hello, there!'

Amalie glanced over her shoulder. On the newly-arrived motor cruiser a red-haired man had come on deck, and was looking at Blake with a beam of pleasure on his face. Then he bent to the hatch, and shouted to someone below, 'Hey, Lucy, guess who's just shown up? Come and say hello to Andro.'

CHAPTER SIX

AMALIE looked at Blake, her eyebrows knitting with puzzlement. At the same time he glanced at her, but not with the expression of someone whose identity has been mistaken. His reaction was difficult to interpret.

After a marked hesitation he said, 'Hello, Desmond. How are you?'

'Fine, fine—in prime nick, old boy. We put in here yesterday and I rang up the house in case you should happen to be in residence, but they said you were off on a cruise and wouldn't be back for some days.'

A woman appeared, her face lighting up at the sight of Blake. 'Andro! You've come back early. How nice. We thought we should miss you.' Her gaze moved to Amalie at whom she smiled before glancing expectantly at Blake.

He said, 'Amalie, my I introduce two old friends of mine, Lucy and Desmond Morley. This is Amalie Heron, for whom I've been crewing for a time.'

Both the Morleys smiled, and said 'Hello.'

Amalie, not smiling, said hollowly, 'How do you do?' She turned her gaze back to Blake. '*You* are Andronicus Androcles?' she asked in an unsteady voice.

'Yes, I'm afraid so. I did once tell you my first Christian name was rather a mouthful.' He was beginning to smile, his blue eyes to glint.

Regardless of the two people watching, she said, 'How could you! How could you make such a fool of me?'

And fled below.

He caught her before she could lock herself in her cabin. A short violent struggle took place, but she was no match for his strength.

159

Holding her immovably pinioned in his arms, the top of her head under his chin, he said, 'I'm sorry you found out like this. I was going to tell you at Paradise, but——'

'But meanwhile it's amused you to let me make an idiot of myself ... offering you a partnership ... telling you I——' She bit off the two final words and burst into tears of despair.

Now there could be no hope of a future together. Before there had still been a slight one, but now that Blake stood revealed as Andronicus Androcles, owner of Paradise, heir to millions of dollars, and a rich man in his own right, there could be no hope at all.

His hold on her did not slacken and, all her control broken down by the shock of finding out who he was and knowing she had lost him for ever, she was helpless against the convulsive sobs which racked her slim body.

He let her weep for a little, her tears soaking into his shirt until he said quietly, 'Hush ... don't cry any more, my sweet girl.'

His sweet girl? She lifted her face, not caring that her cheeks were wet, her drenched lashes sticking together.

Blake—she would never be able to think of him as Andronicus, or even as Andro, the diminutive used by his friends—wiped one of her tears with his fingertip.

'I think you were going to say "telling you I loved you"—although in fact you never did, not in so many words.'

'But you knew,' she said, in a shamed whisper, and would have hidden her face again, had he not prevented her by putting his hand under her chin.

'I knew you thought it was love, but I also knew it might not be. I should never have come and crewed for you. It wasn't fair. I could have made other arrangements when Adelpho's father was taken ill. But because you'd mistaken me for my grandfather's watchdog, I gave in to an impulse to use your mistake as a cover for three or four weeks "away from it all". You see, the privacy which you take for granted is, for people like me, a luxury. Riches are news, and people who have them in abundance are pried on, and envied, and often hated by those who have fewer worldly goods. Cheiro used to say he knew less than half a dozen people whose friendship was untinged by any self-interest, and I'm in much the same case. So being just a man called Blake to you and your passengers has been a holiday for me.'

'What do you mean?—You knew it might not be love?' she asked, in an unsteady voice. To dissemble any longer seemed pointless.

'A young girl can think it's love when it's only Nature ensuring the survival of the species,' said Blake, in his driest tone. 'The test is time, which is why I'm going to go away. If in, say, three months' time, you're still thinking of me, then maybe—who knows?—what you feel at this moment is something lasting.'

'But you'll have gone. You won't know,' she said, very low.

'I may come back, I may not. I have to be honest with you, Amalie. I like you; I want to make love to you. But will it last? I don't know. It never has, but then I've never known a girl like you—unspoiled, unselfish, totally lacking in vanity.'

'I haven't much to be vain about, and especially not at the moment,' she said, trying to free herself.

He held her captive a moment longer. 'Are you going to be all right if I leave you alone for a short time? I shan't be long—say an hour.'

'Yes, yes, I'll be fine. You must go and welcome your friends. I'm sorry I flared at you in front of them. I'm sorry I made a scene,' she said, as he let her draw away.

'You had every right to be angry—finding out who I was in that way. I've been on the point of revealing myself several times, but the last time it was in my mind—the night you insisted on keeping the South Americans on board because of your anxiety to repay my grandfather's loan—your animadversions about me made me think it better to hold my tongue. You said then, if you remember, that you thought I must be much the same sort of man, but on a more de luxe scale.'

'Perhaps you are ... in your real life, when you're not playing the part of "Blake".'

She felt a fresh surge of misery rising inside her and, afraid it might overwhelm her, said quickly, 'I must wash my face. I—I'll see you later.'

But, as she dived into the washroom and closed the door, she did not expect him to come back for several hours, and then perhaps only to tell her he would be spending the night at Paradise.

Later, when she ventured on deck, she found he had finished rigging the awning before going ashore. Perhaps the Morleys had accompanied him to Paradise, or perhaps they had gone shopping. For the present their main hatch was closed and locked, and she could sit on deck without feeling herself the cynosure of curious glances.

Thinking back to the very beginning of their relationship, it amazed her now that she could have missed all the clues to his true identity.

The first one had been the deferential note in the pilot's voice when Blake had apologised for keeping them waiting, and he had replied, 'That's all right, sir.'

An ordinary man, being late, would have come on board visibly rushed. Only a VIP would have left the terminal building with that brisk but unflustered stride, knowing that, although a Concorde might not wait for him, a small inter-island aircraft certainly would. For all she knew, the airline might be privately owned, by him.

Remembering how annoyed she had been with him for bringing two bottles of his own champagne on board, the ghost of a smile curved her lips. It was a small comfort to know that he hadn't been guilty of pilfering, or of lying about his schooling. But why had she formed the impression that it was his mother from whom he had his Greek blood? Clearly his mother must be his English parent.

Which was why, when Amalie had asked him if he were English, he had said, *No, but you are, I imagine.* If his father had been a Greek, Blake would also be Greek by nationality. However, in spite of his claim that his Greek side predominated, it seemed to her that, in voice and bearing, he was as ineffably English as another tall, authoritative man who was by birth a Greek prince.

To her surprise, not much more than an hour after leaving her, he came back. He had gone ashore in the Morleys' tender, but they were not with him now, and Amalie went to meet him in the schooner's dinghy.

As he stepped inboard she said, 'You want to pick up your kit, I expect.'

'No, I want to get on with the turn-round so that we can take some time off together before I go back to Europe. Adelpho is flying in the day after tomorrow, to take my place. I'll stay till your next charter starts.'

'I can manage the turn-round alone as we've come back early. You needn't feel obliged to help. I'm sure you'd much rather relax with your friends at Paradise.'

'We'll both relax with them this evening when we dine *à quatre* at Marguerite's place. I think I did warn you before that Adelpho won't be much help in the galley, didn't I? In his eyes cooking is women's work.'

'I'm amazed that you're able to cook, now I know who you are,' said Amalie, striving for lightness.

'That's my mother's influence. Before she married my father she was one of a large, hard-up family who all took a hand with the chores, the boys as well as the girls. She was always at pains to counteract any tendency in me to sit around and be waited on, as I was when I stayed with my Greek relations.'

By lunch time he had washed the hull. To Amalie, hearing snatches of whistling coming through the ports as she busied herself between decks, or sometimes peering over the side and seeing his brown back glistening with sweat, it was almost impossible to believe that this man, working as hard as if his week's pay depended on it, was so rich he could buy the schooner a dozen times over and never notice the expense.

When they stopped for their usual light lunch, he said, 'You can forget about the lien on *Seafarer*. I've given instructions for it to be cancelled.'

'Oh, no!' she protested. 'It's generous of you—too generous. But I can't accept such a lavish gesture. It would make me uncomfortable.'

'It would make *me* uncomfortable to leave you with that burden on you. Is my comfort less important to you than your own?' he asked her, with a penetrating glance.

She flushed. 'That isn't fair. I would do anything for you—you must know that.'

'Except to swallow your pride for me,' he said dryly.

There was a silence which ended when Amalie said, 'Very well, I accept. Thank you, Blake—I mean Andro.'

'Why not go on calling me Blake?'

'But everyone else calls you Andro, don't they?'

'You're not everyone. Whatever happens in the future, however things turn out for us, you will always be a special person to me.'

'How I wish you were just an ordinary person, instead of who you are,' she said sadly. 'How did you explain things to your friends?'

'I told them the truth—as I usually do, although there have been times recently when I may have seemed to be a liar.'

'They must have been staggered, weren't they? I mean, at your being the crew on a charter boat, even for three weeks.'

'They're certainly curious to meet the girl who induced

me to crew for her. It was rather a fleeting glimpse they had of you before.'

'You said they were old friends,' she said. 'How old?'

'Since prep school in Desmond's case. Lucy I've known since their engagement party. Their eldest child is my godson, but the children aren't with them this time.'

The Morleys, on whose boat they had drinks before taking a taxi to Marguerite's place, were easy people to get on with, and Amalie soon overcame her initial embarrassment because of her outburst that morning.

Much of Lucy's conversation was about her three small children, left at home in the care of a nanny. She seemed to have married straight from school—a finishing school in Switzerland—and Amalie received the impression that Desmond, if not as rich as Blake, was wealthy enough to employ a housekeeper and a gardener so that his wife's domestic responsibilities rested very lightly on her. Yet the cyclamen cotton dress she was wearing was recognisable as an inexpensive Laura Ashley, and there was nothing blasé in her manner. If the Morleys were typical of his friends, perhaps she herself would not be as out of place in his world as at first she had felt she must be, thought Amalie, with a flicker of hope.

After dinner the Morleys suggested going on to dance at one of the island's hotels. But Blake said that, after a night at sea, he and Amalie needed to turn in early. Having dropped the others at an hotel, he told the taxi driver to return to the harbour.

Because, when they reached it, he paid off the driver, Amalie thought he meant to sleep on the schooner. But at the top of the landing steps he halted, saying, 'I'll come down first thing tomorrow and help you to finish the turn-round. Then maybe we'll spend the afternoon sailing with Desmond and Lucy. Goodnight, Amalie. I'll wait here until you're aboard. I expect she's as secure as we left her, but I'd like to be sure.'

'You mean you're going back to Paradise?'

'Yes.'

'What about your things . . . your razor and so on?'

'I have another at the house. There's nothing on board that I need to pick up tonight. I'll collect it tomorrow.'

'You . . . you wouldn't like a nightcap?'

'Not tonight, thanks. I think we should both try to catch up the sleep we lost last night.'

'I don't feel particularly tired, and you don't look it,' she said, searching his face for signs of the fatigue he had pleaded earlier. 'I know you took two watches to my one, but I didn't sleep much when I was off watch.'

'I'm not tired,' he answered evenly. 'And if I come on board with you, I may change my mind and stay, and I don't think that would be a good idea.'

Amalie moved slightly closer, conscious of a fluttering sensation in the pit of her stomach. 'Not even if I do, Blake?'

For an answer he took her by the shoulders, turned her around and, not ungently, pushed her towards the flight of steps.

'Goodnight, Amalie,' he said, on a note of finality.

The night before the arrival of her fourth charter party, by which time she had met the short, thick-set Greek islander whose normal occupation—this she learned from Lucy—was to look after Blake's racing yacht, she was one of the twenty people who dined and danced at Paradise.

Earlier that day she had felt an urge to buy a new dress for the occasion. However, common sense had told her that she didn't need another evening dress, and to try to compete with the other guests she would have to spend far more than she could afford. So she went to the party in the green cotton dress in which she had danced with Blake— but never close in his arms—during the first charter.

She arrived with the Morleys in the car Blake had sent

to fetch them. Lucy was wearing brown chiffon printed with tiger lilies which brought out the reddish lights in her chestnut hair. Taught by Tabitha to recognise such details, Amalie knew that Lucy's tasselled, draw-string evening bag came from Cartier, and the stones on her hair-clip were probably diamonds, not rhinestones.

Tonight the entrance gates to Paradise were open. As the car passed beyond the trees which screened the mansion from public view, every window seemed to be alight, and much of the garden was illuminated by concealed floodlights.

Blake was standing in the doorway to welcome his guests as their cars stopped under the canopy of the white-columned portico. He was casually dressed in a pale linen suit and a dark shirt open at the neck with a vivid silk scarf knotted there. But because she had grown used to seeing him stripped to the waist, or wearing shorts and a beach shirt as he had the other night at Marguerite's place, tonight his clothes seemed more formal than they actually were. She felt that his other persona, Andronicus Androcles, had almost completely reclaimed him.

He kissed her hand when she stepped out of the car, but he had kissed Lucy's, too, and Amalie could not convince herself there was any special warmth in the way he greeted her.

For the first hour or two she saw little of him, and although she knew that, as host, he had to divide his attention among all his guests, she could not help feeling deflated that her share of it was not more than a few introductions to other guests, and a few pleasantries such as he might have exchanged with any of the women present.

She found it difficult to take her eyes off him, and wondered if people noticed how often she could not prevent her glance from turning in his direction, and if they guessed that she loved him and felt sorry for her.

She had been dancing with a pleasant, grey-haired man who had told her he was a retired marine lawyer, and the music had stopped and left them discussing the possibility that whales were of superior intelligence to humans, when Blake came towards them and said, 'Do you mind if I take Amalie away from you, Lars?'

'Certainly I mind, but I will surrender her with a good grace,' the older man said, bowing to her.

Then, at last, she felt Blake's arms round her because he had chosen a moment when the music was music for lovers. Not caring if people noticed and were amused, she closed her eyes, the better to imprint his closeness on her memory.

So intense was her concentration on the feel of his shoulder, his palm, his jawline against her temple, and his long, hard thighs against her legs, that she wasn't aware he was steering her away from the smoothly-paved terrace being used as a dance floor.

It was only when the strong arm pressing her to him was removed before the music had stopped that she found he was opening the door of one of the few rooms not alight and open to guests.

Blake switched on a light and closed the door, shutting out the music and the sound of voices, and enclosing them in unexpected privacy.

He said, 'I have something for you. Close your eyes again for a minute.'

She obeyed and felt him take hold of her left hand, and slip something over the second finger.

'Now you can open them.'

Amalie did so, and drew in a sharp breath of disbelief. On her finger, glowing with all the colours of the spray-bow sometimes seen in the bow wave, was the opal scarab she had seen in a window in Bond Street.

'Oh, Blake, it's beautiful ... *beautiful*—but I can't possibly accept it.'

'Why not, if you like it?'

'*Like it!*' she murmured, tilting her hand to make some of the colours pale while others deepened. Then, coming back to earth again, 'Because it just isn't done to accept presents as valuable as this. How did you get it here? It is the one I saw in London, isn't it?'

'Yes, it is. I'm known at Philip Antrobus, so I rang up to see if they still had it, and arranged for it to be brought out by air.'

'You paid someone to bring it here?' she exclaimed, horrified at the thought of that expense added to whatever astronomical amount the ring itself must have cost him.

'No, that wasn't necessary. A stewardess on this run is a friend of mine, and she arranged for another of the girls to bring it. I think you can forget the conventions on this occasion. There are no strings attached to it. It's something you wanted, which I can very easily afford to give you, and which seemed a suitable memento of my time aboard *Seafarer*.'

She looked up at him, touched almost to tears. Her voice low and tremulous, she said, 'I wish there *were* strings attached to it. I have nothing to give you as a memento, except myself, and you won't take me.'

'You've given me a great deal, Amalie. Three weeks of being incognito, a very agreeable condition for anyone whose normal life is subject to too much publicity. And some very pleasant memories of Stevenson's "blue days at sea".'

'I'm sure you've had plenty of those before.'

'But I've never met a beautiful girl who, not knowing who I was, liked me well enough to overlook several apparently serious flaws in my character. There's only one other woman whom I know likes me for myself, and who would continue to do so in the unlikely event that I ever find myself a pauper,' he said cynically.

'Your mother?'

'Yes.' Clearly wishing to change the subject, he asked,

'Do you understand the significance of the carving on the opal?'

'It obviously represents some kind of beetle. I don't know what kind.'

'It's the sacred beetle which the ancient Egyptians regarded as emblematic of the power of the sun, and which they wore as an amulet to ward off disease and the evil eye. They thought the beetle must be immortal, because the female of the genus *Scarabeus* buries herself with a ball of dung during the hot weather. She feeds on the first ball and then, in the autumn, emerges to find a fresh supply in which to lay her egg. Then she seals up the hole and emerges, as if she'd died and come back to life.'

As I shall come back to life if ever you come back to me, Amalie thought. And the realisation that in less than twelve hours he would be on his way to Europe made her say, 'At least let me thank you in the usual way.'

Although, with the boldness of desperation, she initiated the kiss, it wasn't more than a few seconds before he took over, reacting to the tentative pressure of her lips with a swift resurgence of the passion which had blazed up between them on the beach.

She clung to him, revelling in the fierce demand ignited by her hesitant kiss. But although she could feel his heart pounding as they stood locked together, her softness crushed against his hardness, he still retained enough control, finally, to reach for her wrists and put her away from him, in the same way he had with Hélène, only rather more roughly.

'It's just as well there are people out there, or I might forget my good intentions,' he said, his voice roughened by the desire which still gleamed in his narrowed blue eyes although by sheer force of will he had managed to curb it.

As it was known he was leaving early the next day, the party did not go on late. People began to go soon after midnight and by then, knowing there was no possibility that he would drive her back to the harbour separately, Amalie was almost glad when the Morleys suggested leaving on the grounds that she would want to be bright-eyed and fresh to greet her passengers.

To say goodbye, perhaps for ever, to the man she loved, with other people standing by, called for every ounce of her self-command.

She put out her hand and, chin lifted, said, with a forced smile, 'Goodbye, Blake. Thank you for a lovely party, and for all your many other kindnesses.'

'My pleasure, Mis' Amalie honey.'

That he used this particular designation, borrowed from Marguerite and given by him a half teasing, half tender inflection which made it a pet name, was almost too much for her. Her lower lip trembling, she tugged her hand free of his and stepped blindly into the car to sit next to Lucy while Desmond took his place beside the driver.

For the rest of that interminable night, between fitful snatches of sleep, Amalie's overwrought mind kept de-luding her that she could hear a car arriving at the end of the quay—Blake's car.

Next morning, for some time after she had seen the early inter-island plane taking off into the bright sky, she could not dismiss the hope that, at the very last moment, he might have changed his mind and be coming back to her.

But when an hour had passed, and he hadn't come, she knew there could be no more hope. He had gone, and might never come back.

If he didn't, she knew with dulling certainty that, last night at Paradise, in his arms, she had seen her last glimpse of the heaven on earth which could have been hers—had he loved her.

By the time the Scotts returned from a three-week charter

in the Grenadines Amalie was able to tell them about the changes which had taken place during their absence without betraying any emotion, or so she thought.

Her fourth and fifth charters had passed off smoothly and successfully. Adelpho had proved himself as seamanly as she had expected; his only slight shortcoming being—and this by comparison with Blake—that he was somewhat shy and over-respectful with the adult passengers. With children he could not be faulted and, although he was Blake's contemporary, already he had four of his own, she learned. Troubled that he should be separated from his wife and family on her account, Amalie renewed her efforts to find a replacement for him.

A month after Blake's departure Roderick repeated his suggestion that he and she should join forces.

When she shook her head and begged him not to re-open the subject, his response was, 'Look, I don't want to hurt you, my dear, but it's best to be frank. My mother is convinced that you fell for Androcles in a big way. Is she right about that?'

There seemed no point in prevaricating. 'Yes, I'm afraid I did. Foolish, I know, but ... just one of those things.'

'Poor kid, I know how you feel. I've been through it, too. It puts us both in the same boat, doesn't it?'

'Not quite. You came to realise that you'd been mistaken. I haven't reached that stage yet. For me Blake is still the only man I could ever marry, and I think he always will be.'

'You're too young to say that—much too young.'

Amalie received this in silence. After a pause, she said, 'There's something you don't understand. Blake didn't just say goodbye and walk out of my life. He felt something for me, too, but he wasn't sure that it would last. He left on the understanding that, after three months, he might come back. This is a ... a sort of testing time, for both of us.'

'Has he written to you?'

She shook her head.

'Shouldn't you face the fact that he may not come back? You can't waste the rest of your life because of one unhappy love affair.'

'Do you think I don't face that fact almost every moment of the day?' she exclaimed, in a low but vehement voice. 'Please, Roderick—I don't want to talk about it.'

Most nights, in the slow weeks which followed, she would take the opal ring from its case and, slipping it over her finger, would wonder where Blake was tonight, and if he were thinking of her.

It seemed extremely unlikely. She had been for him merely an interlude; an amusing diversion, swiftly forgotten as his real life in Athens and Paris, New York and London reclaimed him.

She would see, in her imagination, herself many, many years hence: a white-haired, weatherbeaten old woman, still at the helm of a charter boat, and regarded as rather an interesting 'character' by her passengers and other tourists.

If, in that far-distant future, sometimes at night she wore the ring on a finger grown bony and bent, people would wonder how she had come by it, and whether, as well as being single, she was an old maid; or if, a long time ago, in her blossoming days, she had had a lover of whom the ring was a souvenir.

The thought of the empty years before growing old finally quenched her longing for love and for children made her lie in her bunk with tears prickling under her eyelids.

She felt sure that no depths of loneliness would ever drive her into the arms of another man. She was doomed to be forever chaste, unless Blake came back to ravish her.

But he wouldn't. She felt sure he wouldn't. Why

should he want her when a thousand more beautiful women were his at the snap of his fingers?

He had been gone for six weeks when she found a man to replace Adelpho.

Marguerite sent him to see her. He was a South African, nearer to fifty than forty, who, if he could be believed, had once been a senior executive with a large mining company. Then, eight years ago, after a long illness, his wife had died. Having no children, and no longer any ambition, he had taken to a hobo's existence.

Having put him through his paces as a helmsman, and found him as competent as he claimed to be, Amalie made up her mind to engage him when the temporary job he was doing came to an end in two weeks' time. At the back of her mind there was some slight unease at this decision, but she told herself that it was merely that she didn't much like his South African accent, and he bit his nails—neither of which was a rational reason for not signing him on.

At the end of Adelpho's last-but-one cruise with her, they came back to harbour to find a wire waiting for them. It was from the next party of passengers. With apologies, but no explanation, they regretted having to cancel their charter.

'If *Seafarer* is going to lie idle for a week, you may as well go home on the first available flight, Adelpho,' said Amalie. 'There's no point in your hanging about here when you could be with Merope and the children. It will soon be two months since you left them. They must be missing you very much.'

'In four, five days—yes, I go, but first I help you make ready for the people coming next.'

'I can manage alone if I have all next week for the turn-round. You can go home tomorrow, if you can get on a plane.'

But Adelpho came back from the booking office to

report that he must wait three days before returning to his own land. He did not seem overjoyed at his imminent release from a job which could not have been very congenial. Amalie suspected he did not approve of his successor and, being the conscientious type, was concerned about leaving her with him.

For her part, she knew she was going to miss him. He was her last link with Kirios Andronicus, as he called Blake. At first the Greek had been reserved and rarely mentioned his real employer, but lately he had taken to talking about their boyhood exploits together, and, knowing it was probably unwise of her, Amalie had encouraged his reminiscences. Everything he had told her of Blake, in boyhood and manhood, had confirmed her belief that the public view of Andronicus Androcles was as far from the truth of the man as her own idea of him had been.

On the morning of Adelpho's last day with her, he said he was going ashore for an hour, and she took advantage of his absence to wrap up the presents which she had bought for his wife and children. Although it relieved her mind to be sending him home to Merope sooner than he had expected, she could not feel easy about her alternative arrangements.

Suddenly, as she finished tying the last parcel, the misery she had been bottling up inside her for weeks overcame her in a flood of tears. Was it always to be her fate to find happiness only to lose it: first with her grandfather, and then with Blake?

About half an hour later she heard Adelpho coming back on board, and she made a dash for the washroom in case he should call her for something before she had time to wash off all traces of the tears she had shed in his absence.

As she wrung out the wash-cloth and held it over her eyes, she heard her crew come below, pass the washroom and tap on her door.

'I'm washing, Adelpho,' she called out. 'I shan't be more than five minutes.'

He murmured something in Greek, and she heard him go back on deck. She looked at herself in the mirror over the basin, and told herself not to be such a feeble, self-pitying fool again. There were worse things in life than a badly bruised heart.

Her face more or less restored to normal, she went to join him on deck, saying, as she stepped through the hatch, 'Did you get what——?'

The question faltered into silence as she saw who was sitting under the awning.

He rose. 'Hello, Amalie. How are you?'

'B-Blake! What are you doing here?'

'We had an arrangement, if you remember? We would meet again in three months' time to reassess the situation.'

'But it's only two months since then.'

'Yes, but circumstances have arisen which seemed to make an earlier reassessment desirable.'

Oh, God, she thought, with cold terror. He's doing the gentlemanly thing—coming to tell me, face to face, to stop hoping. Perhaps he's met someone else: someone he's sure he wants.

Aloud, she said, 'Oh? What circumstances?'

'One is your decision to replace Adelpho.'

'How did you know about it?'

'He sent me a message. He doesn't think much of your new man.'

'He shouldn't have done that. The new man is perfectly all right, and Adelpho is missing his family. It's not fair to keep him away when someone else is available.'

Blake stepped out from the shadow of the awning into the sunlight. He seemed unchanged; his skin as tanned as before, his eyes as brilliantly blue as when they had parted.

He said, 'That was the secondary circumstance. The primary factor was that I couldn't wait another month. I find I've fallen in love with you, and it's making my whole life impossible. I have to know how you feel. Adelpho has the impression that you haven't changed since I left here.' He put one hand on her shoulder and the other under her chin. 'Is he right about that, Amalie?'

'*Oh, Blake!*' She flung herself at him, her arms round his waist, her face pressed against his hard chest. 'Oh, Blake, I've been so unhappy,' she said, her voice muffled.

'And I.' His arms had closed round her, holding her painfully close. 'I wouldn't have believed it was possible to miss any woman as I've missed you. You've been like a ghost, haunting me by day as well as at night.'

Presently, no longer content just to hold her, he turned up her face and kissed her, regardless of who might be watching. It was a long, hungry kiss such as the one he had forced on her unprepared lips after their first dinner date. But this time, sure that he loved her, Amalie returned it eagerly.

When at last he raised his dark head, his voice was husky as he said, 'So what are we going to do about it? I still can't shelve my responsibilities. There are people all over the world who depend on my companies for their livelihoods, and although I have teams of executives to carry out my policies, the deep driving force is mine. There's something in me which needs the pressure and the challenge of being the man at the helm of a big business enterprise. At this moment I need you more. But I'm too much of a realist not to recognise that, later, I'm going to need that other satisfaction in my life. Can you give up your happy life here to come and share mine?'

'But I'm not happy here without you. I want to come with you,' she answered. 'I don't care where I have to live, as long as it's with you.'

He withdrew his arms, but only in order to take her face between his strong brown hands as he said, 'We shan't have to spend all our time pent in cities. I have a house overlooking the harbour at Hydra, an island not far from Athens. It was built about 1800 by one of my ancestors, a merchant adventurer who made his fortune running the British blockade during the Napoleonic wars. And of course we shall often come here for a few days' sailing on *Seafarer*.'

This reminded her that, before she could start her life with him, she had to fulfil many weeks of charter bookings.

'I wish I didn't have to stay here till the end of the season,' she said. 'How long are you here for this time, Blake?'

'I'm free for a week—and so are you, I believe?'

'Yes, but how did you know?'

'With Adelpho's complicity, I arranged it. The people who cancelled their booking are spending their holiday in my apartment in Athens, with the use of my yacht if they want it.'

'How in the world did you manage to organise that?' she asked.

'As you know, they live close to London. I went to see them and explained that I was going to ask you to marry me, and we needed the week for our wedding and a short honeymoon. It will have to be a very short honeymoon, because I'm sure you would like to have your sister at the wedding, and I know my mother will want to be present. If you're prepared to come with me now, without stopping to pack, we can catch the next flight back to Europe. Adelpho will look after things here.'

'But he's gone ashore, I'm not sure where.'

'No, he's there on the quay, waiting to congratulate me,' said Blake.

Turning her head, Amalie saw the stocky little Greek sitting on a bollard with his back to them. But when Blake called out something in his own language he swung round, grinning from ear to ear.

'But Blake, what about my new crew? The man I've signed on to replace Adelpho?'

'Don't worry, I've already dealt with him. I saw him before I came here, and told him you won't be needing his services after all. He wasn't disposed to argue the matter when I mentioned one or two incidents in his career which he hadn't disclosed to you.'

'You mean he's a crook?'

'No, not that—merely a hell-raiser. He gets fighting drunk every so often. It's not difficult to find these things out if one has friends in the right places.'

'I wasn't too happy about him,' she admitted. 'But I was so sorry for Merope being deprived of Adelpho.'

'The solution to that problem—and also the question of your bookings for the rest of the season—is not to send him back to Europe, but to bring his family out here. Merope is a first-rate cook. She can take over the galley, and the children can live at Paradise, under the eye of my other staff. Now, if it won't take you more than ten minutes, you have time to nip along to *Carrageen* and explain your departure to the Scotts.'

Thus it was that thirty minutes later, with only the clothes she stood up in, which happened to be a pair of emerald cotton trousers and a bright turquoise shirt, Amalie found herself holding Blake's hand as the aircraft roared down the runway.

'Oh, no! I've forgotten the beetle,' she exclaimed in dismay, when they were airborne. 'Your ring—your lovely opal ring! I've left it behind.'

'If you like I can ring Paradise before our next flight, and ask them to keep it in the safe there until we come back. Which reminds me, I have another ring for you.' He produced a small box and, opening it, revealed a large aquamarine surrounded by diamonds. 'The scarab was a memento. This one is a pledge,' he told her, as he slid it to the base of her third finger.

Although flying back to England first class was much more luxurious than the economy flight on which she had reached the Caribbean, the first full impact of the life which was to be hers came outside the airport. Having only hand luggage, they passed quickly through the busy terminal and were met by the uniformed chauffeur of a large, sleek silver Mercedes.

'This is Evans, my driver in England,' Blake introduced him.

'Good evening, miss. Good evening, sir. Your instructions have all been carried out.'

'Splendid. In you get, Amalie.' As she hesitated, Blake gave her a gentle push in the small of the back.

On the wide back seat of the car lay a number of parcels; a large flat box at the bottom, with several packages on top.

As soon as the driver had closed the door and was climbing into his own seat, Blake moved the small parcels to open the big one.

'I hope you're going to like this,' he said. 'If not, we can change it next week.'

He cast the lid on the thickly carpeted floor and turned back the sheets of black tissue enfolding the box's contents.

Amalie gasped as he lifted out a Canadian coyote jacket with a collar of white arctic fox. She had looked at such coats in furriers' windows with Tabitha, and knew they cost not hundreds but thousands of pounds.

'Oh, Blake, it's gorgeous!'

'Try it on. It will keep you warm in this rather sharp wind, and it's a useful, all-purpose coat you can wear with pants during the day or over dresses at night.'

The lining was amber crêpe-de-chine. She slipped her arms into sleeves, and he put his hands under the collar and lifted it close to her chin.

'Yes, I thought it would suit you, and it does. Do you like it?'

'Who wouldn't? It's perfectly beautiful. Thank you, darling.'

She leaned towards him to kiss his cheek, but he intercepted her mouth with his, and the kiss lasted longer than she had intended.

'People will see us,' she said, blushing and pulling away when it threatened to become more impassioned than she thought suitable in public.

'Perhaps I should have these windows replaced with dark ones which can't be seen through, Miss Prim,' he said, with a glinting grin.

She sat back in her corner, stroking the beautiful fur. 'I'm not always prim,' she replied with a touch of coquetry.

'Indeed not! I seem to remember two occasions when you were the reverse.'

Her colour deepened, but the time when she had been unable to meet his gaze for long when his eyes held that particular light was over now. It still sent a tingle down her spine, but it didn't fluster her any more, as it had in the early days of their acquaintance.

'Don't you want to open the other parcels?' he asked.

'Oh, yes, of course. Are they all lovely unbirthday presents? How extravagant you are!'

He caught her hand in a hard grip. 'It's a new experience for me—knowing that, if I couldn't afford to give you anything, you would still have the same expression in those lovely eyes when you look at me,' he said in a low voice, putting her palm to his lips.

The other parcels, when she opened them, contained a scarf of apricot and grey silk by Yves Saint Laurent; a pair of grey kid gloves with silk linings to keep her hands warm; and a big crystal bottle of *Diorissima*.

'How did you know this was my favourite?' she asked, putting some on.

'I recognised it on you the night we had dinner ashore with the Harveys and the Websters. Lilies of the valley are one of my mother's favourite flowers, and she likes that scent.'

'I hope she likes me,' said Amalie anxiously. 'I wish you would tell me something about her.'

'No, it's a mistake to talk about people beforehand. Wait till you meet her.'

'Haven't you told her anything about me?'

'Only your name, and that we're getting married by special licence tomorrow.'

'So soon?' she gasped.

'Did you want to have a longer engagement?'

'No, no—I'd marry you tonight. But such haste must make her very nervous in case she doesn't approve of me.'

'You'll both know the worst in a couple of hours,' he said, with a glance at his watch.

During the flight Blake had told her that while they were airborne Adelpho would have been to Paradise with a message to be Telexed to Blake's personal assistant in London. She would have contacted Tabitha and explained that her sister was coming on an unexpected visit and staying with friends who hoped Tabitha would also be their guest.

When they arrived at the house where Amalie had used to live and her sister did now, Blake waited on the pavement while she mounted the steps and pressed the bell of the first floor flat.

It was not long before she heard footsteps hurrying down the stairs, and then Tabitha opened the door.

'Amalie!' The younger girl's jaw dropped at the sight of her sister's sun-browned and radiant face framed by the fluffy white collar of the opulent coat in place of the well-worn Jaeger reefer in which she had set out from London.

'Tabby!' Amalie hugged her, then stepped back to beckon the man watching their reunion.

'This is Blake, your future brother-in-law. At least

that's what I call him. He's better known as Andronicus Androcles.'

'Andro for short. Hello, Tabitha.' He shook hands with her.

'You're not ... you can't be *the* Andronicus Androcles, are you?' was her response.

'Yes, he is. How did you know about him?'

'Because——' Her sister stopped short, plainly embarrassed.

'I think Tabitha, being a musician, may have taken a passing interest in the gossip-mongers' speculation about my friendship with Calista Livanos, the American pianist, when she was over here last year,' he said dryly.

'Oh, I see. One of your ships that passed in the night,' said Amalie, unruffled.

It was late when they arrived at Blake's mother's home in Hampshire. During the journey he had volunteered one piece of information, which was that she was no longer a widow but had remarried. His stepfather was an Englishman called Michael Gilmour.

Amalie felt very nervous as the car turned off a country road and up a long tree-lined drive bordered by railings with rough grass beyond. Soon lighted windows appeared, the tall, multi-paned windows of a sizeable Georgian country house such as might, for many generations, have been the home of the local squires or lords of the manor.

The sound of the approaching car had been heard within, and before the Mercedes stopped on the gravelled sweep the front door had been flung open and a stout, white-haired man and a woman with a shawl round her shoulders stood waiting to welcome them.

Blake sprang out of the car and kissed the woman on both cheeks before shaking hands with the man. Then he turned and stretched a hand to Amalie.

'Here she is, Mother. Amalie Heron ... soon to be Amalie Androcles.'

'How do you do, Mrs Gilmour,' Amalie said, with a shy smile.

'Oh, but Blake, she's so young,' said his mother, taking Amalie's hand in two thin hands, beautifully jewelled. 'And trembling, poor child. Has he made me out to be a dragon? I assure you I'm not, am I, Michael? Welcome to Westwoods, Amalie. I can't tell you how slowly the time has passed since Blake told us he hoped to bring a bride back with him. We've been on pins with excitement. And this is your sister'—as Tabitha stepped from the car. 'How do you do? Come inside where it's warm, both of you.'

By the time, about half an hour later, that Amalie found herself alone in a pine-panelled bedroom with a four-poster bed hung with ice blue chintz lined with coral, she had forgotten her fears that Blake's mother might not take to her.

Presently, lying in warm water in the adjoining bathroom, sipping the second glass of sherry which Blake had poured for her to bring up with her, she felt she could scarcely be happier than she was at the moment—except that this time tomorrow she would be Madame Androcles, and she and Blake would be somewhere else and alone together.

She was brushing her hair at the dressing-table, preparatory to putting on the white silk shirt and black velvet skirt which had been laid out on the bed—presumably bought by Blake's personal assistant in London who had been responsible for organising the coyote coat and the other things—when there was a tap at the door.

It was Mary Gilmour who entered. She had changed for dinner before they arrived, and was wearing a pale blue cashmere sweater with a soft skirt of the same shade, and a chiffon scarf held in place by an antique brooch.

She said, 'May I come in for five minutes?'

'Please do.' Amalie swivelled to face her, no longer

nervous of the woman who had greeted her so kindly, but still rather doubtful of her own fitness to be Blake's wife.

Mrs Gilmour sat down and, for a few moments, said nothing but merely gazed at her prospective daughter-in-law with a sort of friendly curiosity.

At last she said, 'So you are the girl who, at last, has won my son's heart. I was afraid it would never happen, and that he would miss the best thing life has to offer. I'm so relieved that he hasn't. I've had love twice in my life; first with Lysander Androcles, and now with my dear kind Michael. I don't know how much Blake has told you about us?'

'Very little,' said Amalie. 'At first I thought you were Greek and his father was English, and I visualised you as a little bent, wrinkled peasant. Then I got it right, that you were English, but I still thought you were very poor, or had grown up in poverty.'

'That, like everything else, is relative. We weren't poor, in the sense of being hungry, like people in India. My parents were very hard up because there were seven of us, and a large ancient house in need of constant repair. For the first few months of my marriage I found it quite hard to adjust to a life in which money was no object. As perhaps you will too.'

'I'm sure I shall. Already it takes my breath away, the ease with which Blake smooths every snag. He's like the genie of the lamp in *Aladdin*. But long before I knew who he was, I began to feel very safe and protected because he was there to take charge whenever I needed him.' She caught sight of the time, and added, 'I must hurry and dress. No, please don't go, Mrs Gilmour. I won't be two minutes. You must be starving if you've waited dinner for us.'

When, together, they went downstairs to the drawing-room, Amalie saw Tabitha and Blake sitting together on a sofa. Just for an instant, seeing how lovely her sister looked in a short dress of crimson silk, and how attentively he was listening to her, she felt a tiny prick of the outgrown jealousy. Beautiful, brilliant Tabby was so much more up to his weight than she was herself.

But before she had taken more than one step into the room Blake turned his head towards her and she saw something blaze in his eyes which had not been there until he saw her.

Throughout the happy family dinner party which took place shortly afterwards, she was often conscious of his eyes on her, and she found it difficult to concentrate on the conversation when all she really wanted to do was to gaze at him.

They returned to the drawing-room for coffee and cognac, but when Mary Gilmour offered Amalie a second cup, Blake intervened.

'She's had a very long day and it's time she was in bed. I'll come to the top of the stairs with you,' he added, taking Amalie's hand and drawing her firmly to her feet.

Not at all unwillingly, she said goodnight to the others and left the room with him. As soon as he had closed the door behind them he put his arm round her waist and led her towards the staircase.

'I can tell that my mother and Michael are delighted with you.'

'I hope so. They couldn't have made me more welcome. What do you think of my sister?'

'Rather self-opinionated, but perhaps she'll grow out of it. Not as vulnerable as you. Tabitha wouldn't be nervous of meeting her future mother-in-law.'

'I'm not any more,' Amalie assured him. 'She's a darling.'

'So are you.' As they reached the top of the stairs he turned her into his arms.

'Oh, Blake, is this real? Or am I dreaming it?' she whispered, looking up at the virile dark face above hers.

'It's no dream. This time tomorrow we'll be married,

and I shan't have to say goodnight to you.'

The silk-shaded wall lights dimmed as her eyelids fluttered and closed an instant before his mouth came down fiercely on hers in a long, hungry, scorching kiss.

When he let her go she was panting, her cheeks flushed, her pupils dilated. 'I can hardly wait,' she said breathlessly.

'Nor I,' he agreed, his eyes glittering with a brilliance she had never seen before. Reluctantly, he moved away from her. 'So go to sleep quickly tonight. The sooner you do, the sooner it will be tomorrow.'

He turned and went down the stairs, and she watched his tall figure descending, her eyes soft with love and her heart full of eager excitement.

In the hall, he looked up. 'Goodnight.'

She blew him a kiss, then turned away towards her bedroom.

A little later she heard the others retiring, their voices muted so as not to disturb her. On the verge of sleep, she remembered Blake's last night at Paradise when, with hidden despair, she had said goodbye to him, and thought it might be for ever. Now the wretched weeks in between seemed a small price to pay for the intense joy of their reunion, and the golden promise of the future.

Doctor Nurse Romances

and December's
stories of romantic relationships behind the scenes
of modern medical life are:

ANGELS IN RED
by Lisa Cooper

Staff Nurse Margot Prince had been quite happy with
her career, and the brotherly attentions of Dr. Angus
Wheedon, until the arrival of Dr. Paul Laker. Why
should it all change now?

EVEN DOCTORS WEEP
by Anne Vinton

Joanna had been let down in love, and Simon Rivers'
'rational' plan — for her to marry him and forget her
heartache running a clinic in Tanzania — appealed to
her bruised pride. Then she fell in love again ... with
Simon!

Masquerade
Historical Romances

Intrigue excitement romance

A PERFECT MATCH
by Julia Murray

Louisa married Simon, Lord Winslow, very reluctantly indeed, and she knew that he had only offered for her to preserve the proprieties. So why should he interfere with her innocent attempts to help his unhappy brother-in-law, Henry Landry?

FRENCHMAN'S HARVEST
by Emma Gayle

Helen Caister agreed to visit her mother's old home — a château in the Médoc region of France — only because she had fallen in love with her cousin, Marc d'Auray, and could not refuse his invitation. But Marc cared only for his inheritance and his precious vines . . .